Cowboy Stealing My Heart
Coming Home to North Dakota Book Three
Jessie Gussman

Jessie Gussman

Acknowledgments

Cover art by Julia Gussman
Editing by Heather Hayden
Narration by Jay Dyess
Author Services by CE Author Assistant

Listen to the unabridged audio for FREE performed by Jay Dyess on the Say with Jay channel on YouTube. Get early access to all of Jay's recordings and listen to Jessie's books before they're available to the general public, plus get daily Bible readings by Jay and bonus scenes by becoming a Say with Jay channel member.

Contents

Chapter 1

Communication, extending grace to each other.
- Paula Hurdle from Oxford, MS

The sports car missed his toe by an inch.

Calhoun Powers jerked his head up from his phone. He should have been paying attention. But he'd been eager to let his brother know that he'd found the O-ring they needed at Sweet Water's hardware store and they wouldn't need to order it in to finish the rebuild they were doing on a turbo.

But it was Sweet Water. There was never any traffic. The traffic that they did have took it nice and slow through town.

Not this sports car.

Out-of-state plates.

California.

That explained everything.

Calhoun's lips pursed as brake lights came on, tires squealed, and the car stopped before the reverse lights came on, and it backed up.

He stood in front of his pickup, waiting for the driver to do whatever they were going to do before he hopped in and headed back to the garage.

The car stopped in front of him.

Dude probably wanted directions.

The tinted window slowly went down, and from the angle he was looking at, he saw a long, slender leg.

It wasn't a dude.

He took a step back and lowered his head slightly, looking in the window to meet the eyes of the driver.

Wasted effort, since she wore huge, dark sunglasses, that took up most of her face.

Long golden blonde hair poured down her back and over both shoulders.

There was something familiar...

Calhoun's eyes lifted slightly from the woman, looking over her low-slung car at the movie theater that was directly across the street.

Usually they played movies that were several months old or even older.

But the entire town had been abuzz, along with the rest of the country, about the brand-new romantic comedy that was set to release in the next week.

The highest-paid actress in Hollywood was in it, and her leading man was the man that she just had a one-million-dollar divorce settlement with.

Their chemistry on-screen was supposed to be sizzling, even though they'd been fighting and barely speaking to one another off-screen.

It was such a big deal that the owners of Sweet Water's movie theater had actually bitten the bullet, paid the high fees, and ordered the movie in.

Figuring that even a small theater like them would be able to make their money back on such a huge movie.

The poster for that movie took up the entire front window.

The actress on the poster was smiling coyly and had her finger wrapped around the tie of the actor standing across from her.

The lady in the car wasn't smiling and didn't look coy, but there was something familiar about her, and Calhoun searched the poster for just another second before his eyes dropped back down to the woman in the car.

"Can I help you, ma'am?" he drawled, putting a little more country in his words than was strictly necessary. He wasn't sure why, other than he didn't want her to mistake him for anything other than what he was, which was a blue-collar dude who might be able to work on her car but would never drive one as fancy as that.

He could build her house, but he'd never live in it.

That thought came to him, since he had been renovating the vacation rentals for Rem and Elaine Martinez, one of them just for some big Hollywood hotshot.

Maybe that was this lady.

She didn't bother to lower her glasses, but she did manage to look down her nose at him when she said, "I'm looking for the Martinez vacation rentals. My GPS seems to have quit working."

"It does that around here," he said, and there was no sympathy in his voice. Hard to dredge up any feeling of compassion when she obviously had everything she could ever want at her fingertips.

He ought to know, since he'd spent the last month turning one of Rem's rustic cabins into the lap of luxury. For him, anyway, since it included a jetted hot tub, a massive large-screen TV, skylights, stainless steel appliances, wall-to-wall tile in the bathroom and kitchen, as well as voice-activated lighting and heating.

Each request had seemed more ridiculous than the last, as they came in one by one. Almost as though the woman were changing her mind, needing more and more in order for her to retreat to the country.

"Well?" the woman in front of him said, irritation in her tone.

"Well, what?" he asked, wondering if she thought that he was going to somehow be able to fix her GPS. He wasn't a magician.

"Can you give me directions to Martinez vacation rentals, or should I ask someone a little higher on the evolutionary ladder?"

He grunted, not because he needed to make a noise, but because he clamped his teeth over the "yes" that wanted to come out. Just because this woman rubbed him the wrong way didn't mean he needed to be rude.

He forced a pleasant, if small, smile on his face. "Keep going straight out of town. Just follow this road for about thirty miles. There'll be a right-hand turn and a little wooden sign with white lettering and an arrow. The name of the road is Convenient Marriage, and you'll just follow that back until you see the rentals." He nodded his head in that direction and then figured he'd better add,

"If you need to talk to Rem, you have to stop at the house which isn't far off Convenient Marriage Lane on the left."

The woman pursed her lips and somehow looked like she was smiling and holding her nose at the same time. "Thank you. Do I need to pay you?"

He almost thought she was asking that question as an insult, but he supposed he wasn't sophisticated enough to be offended.

He just shrugged and said, "No."

He had no desire to continue a conversation with her and even less to try to figure out what was offensive about what she had just said.

She looked smug.

She didn't look away, although her finger moved slightly, and the dark tinted passenger window glass slowly closed.

Calhoun didn't wait for it to shut the whole way before he straightened and took a step back, ready to get in his truck and pull out as soon as her car was no longer in his way.

He didn't have to wait for long, as she took off quickly. The tires didn't squeal, but he figured it was just a miscalculation on her part.

Walking around the front of his pickup, he'd gotten a hand on the latch when his phone rang.

Pulling it out of his pocket, he climbed in before he answered. "Hello?"

"Calhoun. It's Rem. I have a favor to ask of you."

"Go ahead," Calhoun said easily. He'd been doing favors for Rem for over a month as the big movie star had been changing orders right and left. Calhoun didn't mind, because Rem was paying him well.

He had been planning on working on the cabins today, but his family had gotten their show truck in the garage, and he was the only one who could put hardwood floor down in the cab. Then he'd gotten roped into a couple of other projects, but he figured it didn't matter, since his dad knew the day after next he'd be moving up to Rem's to work full-time on the cabins over the holidays. Rem wanted them finished before the spring tourist season started, and things were usually slow at the garage over the holidays for his family anyway.

His brother Silas was the one who did all the motor repairs, although Calhoun had done his share of helping, since tearing down a motor and rebuilding it was a lot of work.

His brother Flynn kept the numbers for the company, but he also was the one who did all the painting. It took a steady hand and a ton of patience in order to do it right.

Any carpentry work, including redoing entire interiors, fell to Calhoun. He just had a knack for those kinds of things.

"I got a call from my family in Texas, and I need to go down early. We were planning on going down for Thanksgiving and staying through Christmas and New Year's, but my mom fell and broke her hip, and I'm going to take the family down so we can give a hand on the ranch and also help with her care."

"That's fine," Calhoun said. "I hope she heals up fast," he added, figuring he ought to at least say something along those lines.

"She's tough. I'm sure she'll be fine. But I just want to make sure that you'd be okay continuing with the work that you're doing, and I was also wondering if you might be interested in taking care of my guest. There's just one of her, and as far as I understand it, she wants to be left alone, so she shouldn't give you too much trouble. Of course, you can stay out there like you were planning on doing, living in the big cabin while you're working on the others."

"It definitely makes it easier. I can just get up and go to work. If I'm going to be at some movie star's beck and call, it might be nicer if I don't have to drive forty minutes to get there every time she needs something."

Rem laughed. "What makes you think she's going to be high maintenance?"

"Oh, I don't know. Maybe the fact that she's changed everything she wanted at least four times and has been rather demanding every time."

He didn't mention that he'd met her and figured it was her typical personality to expect the world to wait on her hand and foot.

Rem laughed again. "At least you're getting paid well."

"That's what I tell myself every time. Although, it is kind of frustrating to do a job, only to rip it up and have to do a different job. I think there are mental institutions for people who are forced to do that type of thing."

"Sometimes I think a mental institution would be a nice break from real life." Rem's voice held sage wisdom.

"I guess I haven't gotten to that point in my life, old man," Calhoun said, just rubbing it in that Rem was a good decade or so older than he was.

"The married life, not age," Rem said, then under his breath, he said, "Ouch!"

Elaine said something in the background, and Calhoun laughed. Rem and Elaine had the type of relationship that he would love to have. After more than a decade of marriage, they still smiled at each other and held hands and seemed to admire and respect each other.

It was fun to watch them interact, even though Calhoun wouldn't have called himself much of a romantic.

He wouldn't mind getting married. Settling down. Having someone to greet him when he came home at night. A companion, a friend, someone to walk through life with him.

"I don't mind taking care of things while you're gone. As long as I'm not going to be held responsible when your Hollywood starlet decides North Dakota is too much for her, and she runs back home to the city."

He knew Rem wouldn't hold it against him. Even if it was entirely his fault. Rem was a good man. He would never expect Calhoun to not offend someone who was bound and determined to be offended.

"Yeah. Her payment is nonrefundable twenty-four hours before she arrives, and that's today. So the money's in the bag. Not that I don't think we ought to do our best to give her what she wants. She's paid a lot of money, but after what you've been through the last month, twisting yourself into a pretzel in order to do all the things she demands, I know you're up for it."

Calhoun wasn't sure. It was one thing to do carpentry work for someone who was a thousand miles away.

It was another thing to be woken up in the middle of the night because she wanted him to get an extra blanket out of the trunk at the foot of the bed. Or something equally ridiculous.

Still, Rem had paid him well, and he was sure that would continue, so he supposed he could manage to put up with a little inconvenience.

"I don't want to take you from the trucking company if you're needed there, so don't feel obligated."

"It's good. Things have been pretty quiet, other than this last truck that just came in. It's doing the normal winter slowdown. We'll be hauling feed, but harvest is over and freight slows down until January."

That was the way it was every year, which made it nice in some ways but also made it almost seem like a seasonal job in others, where there was not enough work to keep everyone busy, but there was too much to lay anyone off.

He supposed winter was meant to be a resting time.

"Sounds good. I won't be back until after the new year, but if you can't do it that long, just let me know. Make yourself at home, treat it like it's yours." Rem's words were casual, with the confidence that came from a man who knew he was talking to someone he could depend on.

"Thanks. If I run into any issues, I know your number."

"And you also know how to handle them. I'm not worried about a thing. I trust you."

They hung up a couple minutes later, and Calhoun started his pickup.

It wasn't quite ten in the morning yet. He'd finished the floor and just had a small repair job to do. He could make it out to the resort area tonight, most likely.

He really loved it out where the resort was. There was a beautiful lake, pine trees, rolling hills. Pretty views, and nice and secluded. He'd rigged up some solar panels that provided limited electricity, enough for lights and small appliances. The major appliances—washer, dryer, water heater—were gas.

Some of the cabins which were scattered around the lake were rustic enough to not have any of that stuff, just enough room for a bed. They were perfect if someone wanted to rent one for a fishing trip or just to get away from it all.

But the starlet's cabin had been expanded and fully furnished. And refurnished.

Something told him that she might be a pain in the butt.

But another voice said that there was probably a reason she was trying to get away; her divorce—and all the bad press that had been going along with that—would be one of those things. So maybe she'd just want to be by herself.

He could only hope.

Chapter 2

What's made our marriage last these 41 years is being able to laugh with one another every day.
- Rosemarie from Annandale, Virginia

Bellamy Levine pulled her sports car onto the dirt driveway.

It wasn't hard to see the house that the tall cowboy in town had been talking about. Small by Hollywood standards, it had been recently renovated, with a new porch added and what looked like a brand-new roof over a very comfortable, middle-class home.

Compared to some of the other homes she'd seen in North Dakota, it was huge.

And it needed to be, she thought to herself, as she saw what seemed like an entire classroom full of children running around, along with a large black dog, which walked rather stiffly, like he was old.

This must be the place she needed to stop in order to get her key and directions to her cabin.

The woman had seemed extremely nice on the phone. So nice that Bellamy found herself not liking her. She was distrustful of people who were too nice. People who were too nice weren't really being nice, they were being fake. Then a person found out that they only wanted something from them, and the "nice" person stabbed them in the back the first chance they got.

Maybe she'd been in Hollywood too long.

Although, that's the way it had been growing up in Los Angeles.

Her parents had both wanted to be movie stars. They hadn't wanted to get married. And so they didn't. And Bellamy was pretty sure her mother hadn't wanted to be a mother.

But she had done her duty when she had gotten pregnant.

Bellamy considered herself lucky she hadn't ended up like her older two siblings. Aborted.

Her mother had confessed that one day shortly before Bellamy had graduated from high school.

Maybe her mom had been feeling the empty nest syndrome, or maybe she just had too much to drink.

She often had too much to drink.

Her life as a waitress was a far cry from the life of the movie star she had envisioned when she had moved to Los Angeles from Nebraska.

Regardless, by that time in her life, Bellamy had seen success in commercials and as a body double. Her acting lessons had paid off when she landed a starring role across from Ford Wallace.

He'd ended up being her first husband. Even though he was thirty years older than she.

Pulling to a stop behind the oversized SUV that had all of its doors open as well as the trunk and looked like it was being packed with enough luggage to see the family to the other side of the continent, Bellamy adjusted her sunglasses and got out.

The woman, Elaine, had told her they still used room keys and not the electronic locks that so many other rentals had.

Apparently those locks didn't work very well once the temperature got below freezing. Forget it when they got below zero.

Bellamy shivered, wishing she had grabbed her jacket before she got out. Hearing Elaine say "below zero" when Bellamy had been sitting in Los Angeles in the sunshine looking at her beautiful view of the ocean hadn't meant to her then what it did now.

The temperature got below zero. Unbelievable.

Hopefully that was...sometime other than over the holidays.

Snow? She expected that. Elaine had warned her that sometimes the cabins would be snowed in, and it was likely if it snowed, she might have days at a time where she couldn't get out.

They had assured her they would have someone supervising the cabins and that she could call for any emergencies. That person would also plow the roads, but they explained that they would probably already have commitments, and the cabins wouldn't be their first priority. Especially for just one person.

"Hello! You must be Bellamy," a small, blonde-haired woman said as she strode toward Bellamy, her hand out.

Bellamy thought they were going to shake, but the woman didn't stop, instead wrapping her arms around Bellamy and hugging her.

She smelled like yeast and cinnamon. A sweet scent that made Bellamy long for something, although she didn't know what it was.

It's not like her childhood had contained any yeast or cinnamon.

"I'm so glad you made it. Was your flight okay?" the woman asked, stepping back, but somehow managing to get both of Bellamy's hands in hers, and holding them like they were good, close friends, rather than this being the first time they'd been introduced in person.

"We had some turbulence, but everything went smoothly, and we landed on time." She wasn't sure what else to say. The woman asked the question and acted like she was truly concerned about whether or not her flight was good. Which was odd enough that it somehow kept Bellamy from simply saying, "it was good." Somehow the woman made her want to respond to her warmth and friendship.

Even though Bellamy knew from experience it had to be fake.

"Oh, that's terrible. Turbulence can be so scary. And even worse is if you sit with someone who gets carsick." Elaine's eyes got big, and she shook in mock horror.

"That's happened to me a time or two."

"And me. Flying with children can be a challenge," Elaine said with a small laugh that sounded sweet and happy, and not all fake.

This whole scene could be from the stage or from a movie. Although Elaine's beauty was more of an inner beauty, something that shone out from her, rather than an external cover girl look.

It was an inner beauty that matched her outer actions and seemed to draw Bellamy in without her realizing.

"Well, as you can see, we're packing and getting ready to go. We're leaving a little earlier than we expected because of Rem's mother needing us. But I do have your key right here." Elaine handed her a set of two keys that she pulled from her pocket.

"And I have already emailed you the instructions. They include Calhoun's phone number. Calhoun is the one who will be plowing snow, taking care of any of your emergencies. He also will be staying in the cabin on the other end of the lake. We did so many renovations to your cabin that he wasn't able to get the rest of them finished. I believe we spoke about that in our emails?" Elaine said, and the friendliness was still there, but there was just a hint of business intelligence, like she was beautiful and friendly and sweet, but she knew how to hold her own as well.

Bellamy found herself admiring that, even as she was drawn into it. "I remember. And I'm sorry." She didn't say anything else, although it was tempting for her to want to defend herself.

Her new assistant kept telling her that she didn't want to be in a cabin with no electricity. And she didn't want to not have a sauna. And she deserved to have top-of-the-line luxury for her floors and walls, and Bellamy had been so wrapped up in her heartbreak and trying to play the part of a fun and sassy heroine who was falling in love alongside the man who had brutally—and very publicly—broken her heart and who she had to see slobbering over her ex-assistant, Marissa, whom he had cheated on her with, even while he fought her for everything they owned, that she hadn't cared what her new assistant had insisted on.

Personally, she would live in a hovel, if it meant getting out of Hollywood and away from Houston Park. The rest of the world could swoon over him, but she knew what a lying jerk he really was.

And are you any better?

She hated that voice. It had gotten louder and louder as she got older and lived longer in Hollywood.

People were supposed to sear the conscience, not have it grow legs and start walking around in their head.

I have never cheated, she told the voice in her haughtiest tone.

"Did you get the email?" Elaine's question interrupted the argument she was having in her head.

We will continue this discussion later.

She cleared her throat. "I did. I didn't open it because it came while I was driving."

Not that she never looked at her phone while driving, but today she hadn't. Whatever was happening in Hollywood, whatever her agent wanted, whatever was going on with the movie, she was done.

Though up until two weeks ago, she had attended every single event on her schedule. Because that was the kind of person she was. She didn't quit when things got hard. Even though it meant walking beside Houston, pretending not to hate his guts.

"Thank you. I'll let you know if I need anything."

"Please do. Don't hesitate. We might be in Texas, but we have plenty of friends up here who will help us out and Calhoun is the absolute best. So if you need anything, don't be afraid to ask. You have my number; you have my email. All right?" Elaine prompted, motherly and caring.

"I won't hesitate. I promise."

Elaine smiled like Bellamy's answer satisfied her. Bellamy almost rolled her eyes, because her assistant had not hesitated to "reach out" to Elaine's husband for any renovations she thought Bellamy might need.

Elaine didn't seem to hold that against anyone. Even though Bellamy was almost sure that Abigail had not told Elaine that it was not Bellamy requesting the renovations and changes. After all, a movie star's word carried a lot more weight than a lowly assistant. And Abigail didn't hesitate to use that weight to push her own weight around.

Elaine pulled her in for another hug, and they parted, with Bellamy taking two steps before Elaine gasped behind her.

"Oh! I forgot to tell you, the Piece Makers...uh, the members of Sweet Water's quilting club, and I suppose our unofficial welcoming committee, are out at the cabin now, adding some little touches to make you feel at home. They should be done soon. And shouldn't bother you," Elaine said, although for the first time,

Bellamy got the impression that maybe Elaine didn't have total confidence in her words.

"Thank you for letting me know. It won't scare me now if I get there and there are people in my cabin."

"They're not frightening. They're nice ladies, all very kind and sweet and harmless."

Again, Bellamy got the distinct impression that Elaine was trying to convince herself of what she was saying, but she didn't dwell on it.

With a final wave, she walked to her car and got in.

She was counting on this vacation to heal her heart and her soul and give her peace. It seemed fitting that her welcoming committee would be called the Piece Makers.

Chapter 3

Forgiving one another as often as needed.
- Candy Kennedy from Erie, PA

"I didn't know you had a kid."

Calhoun Powers jerked up, smacking his head on the air cleaner as he maneuvered in the tight space under the hood of the Peterbilt he was working on.

"I don't." His words were short, clipped, as the pain from hitting his head traveled down his backbone and made his fingertips tingle. He should know better than to allow any of his brothers—even Nolt, who was usually steady and not prone to messing with him—to get to him.

The pain had dulled to a heavy throb as he gripped the wrench and worked on loosening the bolt.

"Funny, since there's a lady here—someone we went to school with—who says one of her kids is yours. Figured I'd warn ya, since she's gonna be in here just as soon as Dad's done getting the whole story."

Calhoun had turned thirty last year, but this was one of the drawbacks of working in the business with his dad and brothers—his dad was still a huge influence in his life and sometimes wanted to treat him like he was still a kid.

Although, he supposed if there was a woman there claiming to be the mother of his child, he appreciated his dad "getting the whole story." It would make it easier for him to send her on her way. Hopefully.

His dad's heavy work boots didn't make much sound as they tramped across the smooth cement floor of their two-bay garage, but the lighter click-click of a woman's high-heeled shoes rang much louder.

Maybe it was Calhoun's imagination, but it felt like all work had stopped and his brothers—the three that were in the garage today—were finding a good position to enjoy what they were sure to suspect would be a good show.

Calhoun straightened, careful to move around the air cleaner and not smack his head a second time.

He shifted out from behind the front steer tire and shoved the wrench he held into his back pocket, grabbing the rag he kept there and wiping his hands.

He was an okay mechanic, but he was much better at carpentry and plumbing, and he wasn't a terrible electrician, either. Still, he'd been looking forward to being done here today so he could head up to Rem's cabins for the holidays. After working elbow to elbow with his brothers, the solitude would be welcome, for one.

Calhoun wiped his hands as he walked around the hood of the Pete. Nolt wouldn't hesitate to mess with him, but he wouldn't lie. There was definitely something up, and whatever it was, it was better to face it head-on.

His dad walked toward him. A woman, short, wearing skin-tight leggings with heeled boots and a tight shirt that bulged in various places, walked beside him, her gaze almost militant. Whatever she was going to say, it looked like she was expecting an argument from him.

"Calhoun. I don't suppose you remember me?" she spoke before they stopped just beside the Peterbilt emblem on the upturned hood of the truck he'd been working on.

"No?" He tried not to squint, but she didn't look the slightest bit familiar to him. For a minute, he allowed his eyes to drift back to the three boys who followed her like ducklings behind their mother. All three sets of eyes were wide as they looked around at the shop, with the tools and parts and big trucks in various stages of being gutted and fixed.

The woman rolled her eyes and looked annoyed. "Maci Stallingston. If I say 'midnight tryst behind the bleachers on graduation night,' does that jog your memory?"

He recognized her now—Maci Stallingston. They'd graduated in the same class, which, since their class had a total of thirty-three students, he'd not have a problem remembering everyone.

But trysting behind the bleachers? He'd never done that. Not with Maci. Not with anyone.

He'd made a decision when he'd turned fifteen to wait for the woman God had for him, and while it hadn't been an easy decision, he'd stuck to it.

"I've never trysted with anyone behind the bleachers, but I do remember you from high school, now that I know your name." She looked a lot different than he remembered. Back then, her hair had been dark and there wasn't quite as much of her to notice.

"I figured you'd try to deny it." She reached behind her and grabbed the tallest boy by the shoulders. "This one's yours." She shoved him in front of her like pushing him around was going to get Calhoun to somehow decide she was right.

The kid stumbled to a stop in front of Calhoun, his eyes downcast, his skinny body slouched, not in boredom or disrespect but in a way that made Calhoun think he wanted to disappear.

Calhoun's heart softened.

The garage was stone-cold quiet.

Normally there was pounding, laughing and talking, the air gun thumping and motors running, but there wasn't a sound.

Calhoun swallowed. This was her word against his. All he had to say was the kid wasn't his, and his family, who had never heard him lie, not one time in his life, would believe him and stand behind him. It might end up being a fight with the woman to prove it, but Calhoun knew exactly how it would end—because he'd never done what Maci claimed.

Still, he couldn't help the sympathy and compassion that knocked against his ribs as he stared at the kid.

Couldn't help the feelings that churned in his chest—feelings from having his own mother walk away from him. Feelings of not being wanted and not being good enough to engender the love of his mother. Feelings of failure and worthlessness. It all came flooding back to him at the sight of the boy's slouched shoulders and downcast eyes.

"He's the only one that's yours, but you're taking all three since I've raised him for the last ten years. You can put some extra time in."

"You want me to take two boys that you're claiming aren't even mine?" He couldn't keep the "you're claiming" out of his question. It went against everything he believed to even allow people to think that he had a child. No matter how bad he felt for the boy—for all three boys.

"You haven't helped with this one." Maci pushed the back of the boy's head forward as she indicated she was talking about him. "Not once in his life. So you can make up for lost time."

Her voice was strident. Bossy. Sure.

She wasn't giving him any choices. Maybe she felt she had to be that way in order to get him to do what she wanted. To leave him no space.

And she didn't seem to recognize his irritation with the way she'd shoved the kid like he was an old shoe she wanted him to look at.

The seconds ticked by as Calhoun tried to consider his options.

Fight Maci. Refuse to take the kid.

Or...give in. Take the boy.

Was that even an option?

He was a single thirty-year-old with no experience in raising children and no place to even keep them—he stayed in a room over the garage and didn't even have a house, although he had enough money saved to buy one, just wanted a farm, which took more.

Take him.

I don't have any place to keep him.

You're going to fix up cabins for Rem. Plenty of room for boys.

He hated it when the voice in his head made sense. Usually he figured that was the Lord trying to speak to him, but...did God really want him—someone with zero experience with children—to actually take a boy?

Maybe God wanted Calhoun to have some influence in the boy's life.

With his lack of experience, he could ruin the kid.

Lord?

Take all three of them.

Right. So, why had he asked God again?

I don't know anything about taking care of kids. And I'm busy. I have cabins I promised I'd work on for the next eight weeks.

Take the boys with you. They can watch you and learn.

What about school?

There was no immediate answer to that question, but he did have a distinct feeling that there were some things that were more important than book learning. Some things a kid couldn't learn in a classroom. Some things a boy needed a...dad for.

All three, Lord?

Yes.

Calhoun didn't have any trouble knowing exactly how many boys God wanted him to take.

Still...

"Why do you want me to take all three when you're claiming only one is mine?"

Maci gave an exaggerated sigh and rolled her eyes, the thick, black lines of makeup looking dark against her green irises and making her look like a raccoon. "I told you. You haven't helped with his care up until this point in his life. You'll take all three boys and make up for lost time."

"Mom wants us out of her hair because her new boyfriend wants to go on a road trip on his Harley and she needs to ditch us somewhere." The kid lifted his eyes and spoke resentfully.

Calhoun nodded thoughtfully, letting the boy know he was giving his words serious thought, although he was more interested in the color of the kid's eyes. Brown. Dark, almost black.

Interesting since Calhoun's own eyes were blue. Although he'd heard of two light-eyed parents having a brown-eyed child, the odds were...very, very slim.

But even as he was thinking that, the kid gave him a last glance, then looked back at the floor, like he was sure Calhoun wouldn't want him any more than Maci's new boyfriend. Like he'd given up even thinking he was worth wanting. Like he was trying hard not to care that his mom was basically telling a stranger to take her kids.

"I'll take them. But that's it. I want them forever." Calhoun clamped his mouth closed. Where had those words come from? He didn't even have a house.

Although he was leaving for Rem's tonight, and it was true that he'd have a cabin until the beginning of January.

He'd surprised Maci because her brows shot up, and for the first time, she appeared to be speechless.

He'd surprised himself. Those words definitely hadn't come from him. Which made him all the more sure it's exactly what he was supposed to do, as much as he really, really didn't want to.

He didn't wait for Maci to speak again.

"What's your name, son?" he asked, deliberately using the word "son" even though he knew, beyond a shadow of a doubt, the boy wasn't his biological son.

"Calvin." The kid had jerked his head up with Calhoun's statement about wanting them forever, and when he said his name, his voice seemed to hold hope.

"I'm Calhoun," he said, holding out his hand.

Dark brows drew together as the kid looked at Calhoun's hand like he'd never seen one before.

"It's a little dirty since I've been working all morning." Calhoun figured that probably wasn't the kid's problem, but it gave him a little time to realize that an adult actually wanted to shake his hand.

Calvin straightened a bit, then his hand came up, slowly, and carefully gripped Calhoun's.

Calhoun bit back a smile, keeping his look serious.

"Well, I'm glad you guys can get to know each other." Maci's voice cut into the silence of the garage. The hopeful look on Calvin's face shut down. Calhoun bit back a nasty comment.

"Finally," Maci added, about ten seconds too late for anyone to believe that she'd longed or even thought about the day Calhoun would meet his "son." "Boys. Go get your stuff. You'll be staying with Calhoun for a while."

"What about school?" Calhoun's dad spoke up from where he stood, a respectful ten feet away.

Calhoun appreciated him asking and figured since he'd raised all of his kids while traveling around the country, he'd know it wasn't going to be easy for Calhoun to enroll kids that weren't his and he didn't have custody of.

"We've been homeschooling. They each have a couple of books." Maci's tone didn't hold an ounce of concern, and Calhoun figured it was parents like that—who used homeschooling when they didn't want to be accountable to a schedule or have to stay in one location—that gave homeschooling a bad rep. "Make sure you get those, boys," she said with even less authority in her tone.

Calhoun didn't move, watching as the boys filed back out of the garage the same way they came in.

"I'm glad you're doing your duty and I didn't have to take you to court over it." Maci had completely ignored his statement that he wanted them forever and was back to acting like he was some kind of deadbeat dad who didn't want to take responsibility for his actions.

He felt like the situation was actually the exact opposite, but again, there just wasn't any point in splitting hairs.

"I was serious. I'll take them. All of them. But I want them for good."

He wasn't sure why that was so important to him. Maybe because they just looked so pathetic, like no one wanted them. And he could relate, because his mom had left his family. Just left. And for the longest time...man, who was he kidding? He still felt unwanted and still wondered what was wrong with him that his own mother hadn't wanted him.

Those poor boys had to know the exact feelings he'd had. Their circumstances were a little different, but the idea was the same—all of them were unwanted by their mother.

Calhoun had at least had his father. If he hadn't, he might have ended up as some kind of delinquent or in prison or dead. Probably.

But his dad had stepped up, and while he hadn't been the most considerate or nurturing person in the world, he'd done his best to give his boys discipline and a purpose, if not love, and they'd all turned out to be hardworking and honest, if slightly messed up.

If he'd learned anything through that experience, it seemed like God was giving him the opportunity to show it.

Maci's face had run a gamut of emotions—shock and surprise, suspicion, excitement, and back to suspicion—while Calhoun waited.

He had no idea what he would do with three boys for the rest of his life, but for some reason, that's exactly what he wanted.

"I can't just give my kids to some random stranger."

"I'm not a random stranger. I'm the dad."

"Of one."

"But you're having me watch them all. That's what I want. All three."

"You're getting them. But you only get them for the winter. I have some things I have to do." Her eyes dropped, and he figured she didn't want to say she was going biking with her boyfriend. South, if he had to guess, since it was really too cold for motorcycles in North Dakota in November. Maybe Florida. Texas. Mexico, even.

What would he do if he had to reach her?

"I need some kind of paper stating I'm a legal guardian. In case any decisions need to be made."

What else could come up? Ten minutes ago, kids weren't even on his radar. He couldn't believe in that short amount of time, he'd gone from childless by choice to fighting for—was it custody?—of kids that weren't even his. Guardianship.

"I don't know if I'm sticking around that long."

"You need to. If there are any accidents or sicknesses and I can't get a hold of you…"

"Here's my number." She rattled her number off, finished before Calhoun even got his phone off the toolbox where he'd set it before he'd started working on the truck.

He got the first six numbers in, guessed on the last four, and read it back.

"That's right. You always were a smart one."

He was just good at guessing, but he didn't say that to Maci. Or maybe he was book smart. He wasn't sure. He'd never stayed at a school long enough to win any awards for his brainpower, anyway. Not that it mattered, because when a person got out in the real world, smartness wasn't the deciding factor in success. He'd been around long enough to figure that much out at least.

It was on the tip of his tongue to ask her if she wanted his, but he sent her a text instead, making sure she had it.

Chapter 4

Communication and being a good listener, as well as mind-fulness and mutual respect.
– Kai from Rhode Island

"You really want the kids, like, permanently?" Maci asked, lowering her voice and looking around.

"Said I did." He kept his face from giving away any hope her words had engendered in him. Maybe by the time he'd spent several weeks...months?...with the boys, he'd be ready to give them back, but the idea that the poor kids didn't have anyone who wanted them stirred up every fighting instinct in his body. Every kid should know the security of having parents who loved them.

"I'll give you guardianship, and you watch them for a bit while I...get my stuff done...then we'll talk when I come back."

He hadn't really thought a mother—no matter how terrible a mother she was—would actually just show up, drop her kids off, and sign away her rights to them. Not really.

What she'd just offered was probably as good as he was going to get.

"There's a lawyer in Rockerton. He might be willing to draw something up last minute like this."

Calhoun didn't know anything about guardianships, but he figured they at least required a lawyer.

"I'll see if Bobby'll stop there." She looked at her phone. "The office is probably still open."

"Yeah. Look it up online. If you call, he might stay late."

Bosman Powell probably wasn't even in the office. He'd be out on his ranch. He came into town when clients called and needed him. He'd only been practicing law in Rockerton for a couple of years, but he was a local and knew most people in the area didn't keep city hours. Neither did he.

"A lawyer that stays late?" Maci rolled her eyes. "Someone's going to pay for that." She gave him a considering look.

Calhoun hesitated. He wanted the kids to know they were wanted, but did he want it so bad he was willing to pay for it?

"You tell Bosman I'll settle up with him." He'd have to go in and sign a ream of papers, most likely, anyway. It might even involve Rebecca Baylor, the judge.

Maci's eyes widened, then narrowed. "What is wrong with you?" she asked, looking like she hadn't wanted the words to come out of her mouth—probably so she didn't shock any sense into him and make him change his mind—but definitely looking curious as well.

"Guess I just don't share very well."

That was true; he'd always wanted things to be just his. Maybe that's the reason he'd made the vow to God to wait for the right girl—he wanted his girl to have waited for him as well. He most definitely didn't want to share his wife, even her memories. He wanted her to be just his.

And just like that, a thought occurred to him: taking these kids permanently might really crush his chances at finding a mate. After all, he'd been looking for a woman who would be his and his alone. It made sense that the woman he was looking for was the same. And with three kids toddling around behind him, it would be obvious—although wrong—that he had a lot of history and baggage.

Lord?

God didn't need to answer. Calhoun knew that sometimes God's ways weren't his, but in this case, Calhoun had been firm. His woman would be all his, or he wasn't interested.

"Son?"

His dad's voice cut into his thoughts, and he turned. At some point in the conversation, he'd forgotten his dad and brothers were even in the shop. Maci had too, if the surprise on her face was any indication.

"Yeah?"

"I'd like a word with you."

His dad didn't wait for him to answer but turned and started walking toward the little office. Calhoun made eye contact with Maci.

"I can't wait around. Especially if I'm gonna make it to the lawyer's today. I'm leaving." She lifted her chin, as though daring him to contradict her or stop her. But she was wasting her time. He had zero plans to stop her or argue. Even less when he saw that the kids were lined up against the wall on the inside of the door, backpacks and a couple other odds and ends at their feet, their eyes glued on the adults that were going to determine their fate.

The oldest boy—had he said his name was Calvin?—stood with his arm over the shoulder of the shortest one who leaned back against his big brother. The sight tore at Calhoun's heart. What kind of mom could put herself ahead of her children like that?

A dumb question, since people were told to put themselves first, take care of themselves first. Some people went overboard, since the idea of putting others first wasn't taught or encouraged.

"That's fine. My brothers will keep an eye on them until I'm done talking with my dad."

He didn't need to ask. They would. It wasn't the first time they'd had kids in the shop, and they'd make sure no one got hurt.

Calhoun walked into his father's office, Nolt following on his heels and closing the door behind him.

Maybe because Nolt was the oldest, or maybe because he just had a commanding way about him, but neither Calhoun nor his dad questioned his presence nor acknowledged it.

His dad barely waited for the door to close before he started speaking.

"Those kids aren't yours."

A tight ball that Calhoun hadn't even noticed relaxed inside of himself. He'd believed, truly believed, that his father would believe him. Would not question him. But there must have been some part of him that worried he would.

He almost smiled.

"I know."

"She's using you."

"I know."

"What are you thinking?"

His dad didn't have to say any more. Calhoun could read between the lines: *Kids are a lot of work. That's a lot of responsibility. She'll end up leaving and never coming back. When you take children, you're not taking them for the day, the responsibility lasts a lifetime.*

Yeah. His dad didn't have to say any of that. All that had been going through Calhoun's mind as the strange words had been coming out of his mouth.

While he was still grappling for a way to explain to his dad what was going on in his head, Nolt spoke.

"If Calhoun hadn't said he would take them, I would have."

His dad's eyes flew to Nolt, brows shooting up his forehead, his whole facial expression just screaming that he had no clue what had gotten into his boys.

Calhoun turned his gaze toward Nolt, who was staring at him, his eyes boring into his, his whole expression saying that he understood.

"Growing up, we were the boys whose mother didn't want them. No one wanted us. We know just how those guys feel. No kid should have to feel like that. They should know that there is someone in the world who wants them. I think every single one of us standing out there in the garage were behind Calhoun hundred percent. And if he hadn't done what he did, we would have."

His dad's mouth opened and closed. Then opened and closed again. Then his dad rested his hip on his desk and crossed his arms over his chest. "I can't help what your mother did. I'm a little offended that you're lumping me in with her."

"I'm not." Calhoun spoke up immediately. Nolt murmured in agreement, then quieted and allowed Calhoun to speak. "That's what Nolt was saying. Our mother didn't want us, but you did. That's the only thing that saved us. But those boys don't even have a dad to stand up for them. Somebody had to."

"So that's why you said you wanted them forever. Because you want them to know how much you want to help?"

Calhoun wasn't sure he would put it like that, but he didn't know how else to say it, so he crossed his arms over his chest and nodded.

His dad nodded slowly, his look thoughtful. "You could foster them. Let the state find someone who actually wants them. I'm pretty sure the government might have something to say about a mother who would drop kids off with a strange man and go off biking with her boyfriend for Lord knows how long."

"That's just it. The government isn't a parent. And foster parents are paid. They might really care. Most of them probably do. But it's not the same when you're getting paid to keep a kid versus wanting them. Rearranging your life for them. Keeping them because you love them." The last words were soft, because with his dad and his brothers, as much as he knew they all loved him and would do anything for him, support him in anything, they didn't really talk about love too much.

It wasn't something that they'd grown up doing, and while Calhoun figured he had the capacity to love, he probably didn't have the capacity to be all mushy and gushy about it.

Or sentimental.

His dad's position hadn't changed, but it was obvious that the wind had gone out of his sails.

"I hadn't realized how much that affected you." His eyes shifted to include Nolt. "All of you."

Calhoun shrugged, not looking at Nolt. He probably did the same. There wasn't anything they could do about it. Not for themselves. But they couldn't see it happening to other little boys and not remember their own feelings of inadequacy, rejection, and pain.

Even if they wouldn't admit them.

"It's over. Nothing anyone can do about it. Just when I see it happening, I can't just stand there and let it."

"You can't stand around waiting for someone else to do something." Nolt's voice held no emotion, which almost made it more emotional. There was no doubt in Calhoun's mind, if he hadn't come forward, Nolt really would have. Or any of his other brothers.

Their dad hadn't raised them to stand on the sidelines watching life. He also hadn't raised them to only be concerned about themselves.

They could hardly get upset about injustices if they weren't doing something about those injustices. Getting upset didn't solve anything.

As though Nolt could read his mind, he said, "Maybe if fewer people got upset, and more people did something, actual constructive things that actually help solve problems, there wouldn't be so many."

Calhoun knew exactly what he was saying. Protesting didn't solve anything. Nor did whining. Nor did burning and looting. People who did stuff like that were just looking for an excuse to break laws. They weren't solving any problems.

"You can't solve the world's problems yourself." His dad's tone was reasonable.

He knew it. But he could solve the problem that was right in front of him. The one that God gave him. Take the opportunity that the Lord had opened up right in front of him and use it. If everyone did that, there'd be far less problems to solve. In fact, maybe none.

He shrugged. "I'm not trying to solve problems. I can't save all the world's kids. But when God drops three into my lap, I can hardly shove them aside and keep doing what I want to and ignore what God gave me to do."

Calhoun wasn't sure where those words came from, but they were the truth. There was no doubt that God had given those kids to him. Even if it was because Maci lied about the oldest being his. In fact, maybe that was part of being humble, allowing someone to lie, not correcting them, and being humble enough to do what was right in the situation. Rather than argue and insist on proving she was wrong.

"She lied about you!" his dad exclaimed in frustration.

"Sometimes people miss opportunities because they're too proud. They want to be right. We can allow lies to go unchecked. Policing liars is not our job. Our job isn't to correct every lie or wrong statement. Our job is to see what God is wanting us to do and do it."

Nolt put a hand on Calhoun's shoulder. "I admire your humility."

Their dad shook his head. "Sometimes I can't believe I raised you boys. You guys are absolutely right. It's my pride that's bristling about this. I don't want to let the woman have her way, because I know she's lying, and I want to correct her. But that's my pride, and I'm missing the point, which is the children." Their dad nodded his head. "You guys are right," he said again and grunted a little laugh. "I guess I brought you in here to make you see my point of view, but you wound up talking me into yours. Now, all I need to do is show the same humility you are and keep my mouth shut when we go back out there. I guess, if you're going to have three boys, I'm their grandpa."

Calhoun grinned, even though he hadn't thought that far ahead. There were probably a lot of things he wasn't thinking, but he loved that his dad was going to be fine—not just going to be fine but going to lend his full support.

"Thanks." It meant a lot.

"I think it's going to take a court hearing to get custody. If my memory serves correctly," their dad said, pushing off the edge of his desk, dropping his arms.

"Then I guess I'll be going to a court hearing."

"Humph."

"Rebecca Baylor is the judge. She's not going to need references for Calhoun," Nolt said confidently as he grabbed the doorknob and opened the door.

Chapter 5

1. Putting God first.
2. Marriage is not a 50/50 proposition; it is a 100%/100% or
it will not thrive!
3. The old adage- Do not go to bed angry at one another is
true.
- Lana Burton from Ardmore, OK, born in Ft. Worth, TX,
raised in Decatur, TX

Calhoun opened the diner door, letting the three boys file in first before he walked in, allowing the door to close behind him, the bells jingling. He didn't recognize the waitress—Patty's Diner had gone through several in the past few months as she'd let the regular waitress go in order to hire her niece who lasted maybe two weeks.

Calhoun nodded as the unfamiliar woman looked up and led the boys to a table in the corner.

They silently filed into their seats. The oldest, Calvin, sat with the youngest whose name was Cayson, while Cruz, the middle boy, slid in against the wall and Calhoun sat down beside him.

The waitress was already with a customer, so Calhoun figured they had a little bit of time before she came over.

After Maci had left, he'd gotten the boys' names and their ages, ten, eight, and seven. The boys had hung quietly back in a corner of the garage while Calhoun had finished the job he'd been doing.

They smiled shyly when he'd invited them up into the cab of the truck to ride along for the short ride to the parking area outside.

Maybe Calhoun would have been better off allowing Nolt to claim the children. They seemed to really enjoy being in the garage, and that's where Nolt would be all winter.

Regardless, that's not the way things went down, and Calhoun figured he wanted to get to know them.

"Are you fellas hungry?" he asked, not sure exactly what he should say in order to get to know them. *Hey, I want to get to know you, so tell me all about yourselves* seemed a little...too much.

Although they were children. Maybe that line would work.

Three heads nodded eagerly. Cayson's eyes were bright and excited. He seemed to be the most precocious of the three. Naturally, probably, since he was the youngest.

Although, Calhoun figured he would be the most likely to miss his mother too. For the same reason.

"Our waitress will bring us menus, but it's basically hot dogs and hamburgers, and they have some pretty decent mashed potatoes and meatloaf here. Any of that sound good?" he asked them.

"You mean we can get anything we want?" Calvin said timidly.

"Sure can. And I'm paying," Calhoun said, grinning and winking, although the boys didn't smile, making Calhoun wonder if the adult paying had always been a given in their lives before this.

"What's the cheapest?" Cruz asked, as though he'd been told to order the cheapest thing before.

Calhoun was taken aback a little. But he supposed that made sense. If their parent was hard up for cash but still needed to feed their kids away from home, it would make sense to have them order the cheapest thing on the menu.

But he had been single his entire adult life and had plenty of money saved up. While he had no intentions of going on a wild spending spree, he could afford to feed the boys whatever they wanted, from this menu at least.

"You don't need to worry about what things cost. I've got this covered. If we get to the point where we need to think about it, I'll let you know. Okay?"

The boys looked at him suspiciously, and Calhoun figured that maybe they were used to the adults in their lives not keeping their word. There didn't seem to be much point in making a deal if the person you were making it with wasn't going to keep their end.

That thought made anger flare in his chest. Kids shouldn't have to wonder if they were being lied to. But these boys would just have to learn that when he said something, he meant it.

It would take time and experience.

Nothing he could do about it now.

"Hey there, fellows. What can I get you to drink today?" The waitress came over to their table with a smile, setting menus in front of them.

"I'll take a water," Calhoun said, noticing the woman's name tag said Trella. "What will you fellas have?" he asked, looking at the boys.

"Is there something I don't know about?" Trella asked conversationally, lifting her brows at the boys. She wasn't being nosy, exactly, but while Calhoun didn't know her, she probably knew him, or at least his family, and none of them had three boys.

"They're my boys," Calhoun said easily, knowing as he did Trella was likely to question him.

"You have kids?"

He hadn't quite figured out what he was going to say, so his words came off the cuff, because he didn't want to hesitate and give the boys the idea that he didn't consider them his. Or worse, that he didn't want them.

"Sure do. Calvin there is my oldest. Then there's Cruz, and Cayson's my youngest."

Trella's eyes narrowed, and it looked as though she thought maybe he was playing some kind of game. But she didn't question Calhoun about his history or how he'd acquired three boys since the last time she'd talked to someone about his family.

All three ordered water. He wanted to tell them that they could have whatever they wanted, but he figured water would be just fine. He'd heard that soda could make kids hyper, and although he hadn't experienced it, he figured water was probably just as well.

After the boys had been with him awhile, maybe once they had the guardianship settled, they would have to establish some ground rules. He'd probably have to limit sugar and soda and sugary sweets in general.

Man, all these things he hadn't thought about. He'd have to make...rules.

Surely these things would shake out on their own.

The waitress bustled away, and he looked at the boys. Their eyes were downcast.

"Are you guys able to read the menu?" he finally asked, the idea just coming to him. They seemed like they should be old enough to read, but what did he know?

"I pretty much can. But Cruz and Cayson can't read at all."

"At all?" Calhoun asked, calculating his head. They were seven and eight. Most kids learned to read in kindergarten, right?

Something close to panic started to grow in his chest. He hadn't considered that he might be biting off an education problem when he'd agreed to take the boys.

Not agreed. Demanded.

Regardless, the talk with his dad had solidified the idea in his head. There was no doubt in his mind that God had sent these boys to him. If there was an educational problem that needed to be addressed, God would give him the wisdom to figure it out.

"Cayson knows his letters. And Cruz can read smaller words. But Mom didn't do school with us, she just put books in front of us, told us to figure it out on our own. I helped them as much as I could." Calvin's mouth snapped closed, and he looked down at the table as the waitress came back.

The boys all got hot dogs and fries, while Calhoun ordered a hamburger, even though he had pretty much lost his appetite.

He hadn't considered that he might have to teach the boys how to read.

He waited until after the waitress left before he said, "It's a good thing I have you, then. Because my mom taught me to read, and she made it fun. So I'll do the same with you."

"You were homeschooled?" Cruz spoke, his head snapping up and his eyes interested.

Calhoun nodded. "All my brothers and I were. Mostly. We moved around too much for us to go to school most of the time. Although, I did spend time in classrooms."

"So you were both?" Calvin asked.

Calhoun nodded.

"Just like us!" Calvin said, looking at his brothers as though for confirmation, and both of them nodded back at him.

Calhoun wasn't sure whether to take this opportunity to let the boys know that his mom had deserted him too. That he knew what it was like to not be wanted and to have someone he loved walk out on him.

Maybe it would have helped. Maybe not, but he couldn't find the words and thought maybe that was too much sharing too soon.

It didn't feel comfortable anyway.

Maybe it never would.

"Are you really going to keep us?" Cruz asked, the excitement fading from his eyes and concern replacing it.

"I'm going to try." Calhoun glanced around at the boys. "Is that okay?" He supposed they were young, but they still deserved to have a little say in what happened in their life.

"I guess. I wish Mom wanted us. When she has a boyfriend, she acts like we're a big inconvenience." This seemed like a big word for Calvin. He stumbled over it a little, but Calhoun knew what he meant. And he was perceptive, because he was probably right. When his mom had a boyfriend, they *were* an inconvenience.

"I can't make her want you. But I can guarantee you that I always will." Those were big words, and as they left his mouth, Calhoun prayed that they would be always true.

The boys didn't seem impressed with his declaration. They didn't say anything.

Trying to figure out what in the world they might be interested in, something they could all talk about, Calhoun finally decided that he'd just start out with what they were going to be doing.

"Have you boys ever built anything?"

"We built derby cars one year for a church activity. Although Mom's boyfriend at the time did most of the work, because he said we were too little to know how to put a car together right."

"I see." Calhoun adjusted himself in the seat so he was angled toward all three boys. "You all saw me in the garage today. That's what my family does. That, and the feed mill. But for the winter, I've been hired to finish the interiors of some vacation cabins a little ways west of here. I have a place to stay myself, and—"

"You're not gonna send us to school?"

"I think maybe I'll see what I need to do to homeschool you at least until next year. We'll see if we can't get moving on this reading stuff. I think once you catch the hang of it, you're gonna love it."

"I don't think so. I hate it," Cruz mumbled, and Cayson nodded along. "Reading sucks."

Tempted to tell him that "sucks" was a word they weren't going to be allowed to say, Calhoun let it slide for the time being.

"Don't you guys love stories?" he asked.

"Movies on TV are cool."

"Did your mom ever read to you?"

The boys' eyes rose. They looked at each other, then they slowly shook their heads.

Calhoun's heart sank. This might end up being harder than what he thought it was going to be.

The waitress brought their food as his phone buzzed in his pocket. He pulled it out, glancing at the text.

The judge scheduled a hearing for this afternoon. If you can come, we can get this settled today. 3 o'clock.

That was one of the awesome things about living in a small town. Things had a tendency to happen quickly. Rebecca Baylor was a no-nonsense judge, fair, honest, and she probably saw right through Maci. She'd want to get the guardianship thing settled before Maci skipped town.

I'll be there.

He sent the text and then realized he didn't know what he was going to do with the boys while he was gone. He could hardly take them with him. He didn't want to put them through that, watching as their mom signed away guardianship, then left without a backward glance.

It had been hard enough for the boys to see her drive away the first time, although none of them had cried.

As he thought about it, Calhoun realized his brothers would keep them. His dad would, too, for that matter.

Sure, from now on he was going to have to think about what he would do with the boys anytime he had something he needed to do and he couldn't take them with him, but he had family he could depend on. Even if it wasn't the traditional kind of family.

Smiling a little but careful to keep it to himself, he thought about how he had had no idea how his life was going to change this morning when he got out of bed.

For some reason, a sports car, an elegant nose, and a lilting voice cut through his thoughts.

He wasn't going to be seeing her again most likely. They might run into each other in passing, as he was out there working, but a woman like her would be sure to avoid children and definitely wouldn't mingle with the help.

He put that thought out of his head and concentrated on his boys and their food. He had bigger things to worry about than a spoiled movie star he would probably never talk to again.

Chapter 6

We learned love from the author of Love , Our Lord and Savior. He is ever true, loving , forgiving, comforting, faithful and protective. We married at 19 and weathered the storms together with God's help. Now 63 years, we have only grown in faith and love. We have been truly blessed.
- Maxine Ballard

"Father forgive us for we have sinned."

Charlene stood in the basement of the church in Sweet Water, North Dakota, with her friends and fellow Piece Maker members, Vicki and Kathy and Teresa, holding several pieces of pipe and various pieces of electrical wire.

Her friends held the same in each of their hands, and they whispered softly, repeating what she had just said.

Maybe this was taking their matchmaking efforts a little too far, but with what they had done to the cabin that Bellamy Levine had been planning to stay in, it would be uninhabitable for a while.

Possibly until spring if the pipes froze.

"I feel like I should feel guiltier than what I do. I actually feel...satisfied. Like you do after you've done a full day's work." Charlene looked around at her group of friends. She wouldn't confess that to just anyone. But they nodded, like they knew exactly what she was talking about.

"It's practically a sin for a man like Calhoun to be as old as he is and not be married. We're just correcting a grave injustice," Vicki said without a hint of a smile. She truly believed what she was saying.

They'd almost gotten caught. Bellamy Levine had arrived at the cabin just as Kathy was pulling the last of the wires from the light in one of the upstairs bathrooms.

Charlene was almost positive Bellamy didn't suspect a thing. After all, their welcome basket containing fruits and nuts was sitting on the kitchen bar island, and their additional basket of essentials—dishwasher detergent, paper towels, and hand lotion—was right beside it.

Vicki had insisted that they include another, smaller, box of popcorn, the old-fashioned kind, along with an assortment of herbal teas and a jar of honey. She said even movie stars needed to splurge on good food once in a while. They put two pounds of butter in the refrigerator, since that's what Vicki insisted Bellamy would need in order to make the popcorn edible. Along with a full canister of salt.

They also laid a quilt with a decorative bow so Bellamy would know it was hers on the table behind the couch.

"Bellamy Levine deserves a good man. She's had a bad rap, but a good man will bring out the best in any woman, and there's a lot of good in her." Kathy nodded as she spoke. "I know we did the right thing. Even if it was wrong."

Charlene looked at the pipe and wires in her hands. The right thing, even if it was wrong. That might be a weird way to put it, but she had to agree. In fact, she couldn't agree more. They had done the right thing. Even if it was wrong.

She'd bet money on it.

Chapter 7

A marriage with caring, love, communication and respect from both people will last a long time. My husband and I were married for 13 years and 6 months when he passed away from cancer (April 13, 2017). We talked about everything. Nothing was off limits. It was so much better talking about it, then letting it build up.
- Cindy Hunt from Iowa

Bellamy Levine sat in a rocking chair on the front porch of her new cabin. Home for the next two months. She'd rented the entire vacation spot. Although, from what Elaine had said, none of the other cabins were habitable aside for one, on the other side of the campground, where the caretaker would be staying as he fixed up the rest of the cabins.

She could barely see his cabin from where she sat because several large pine trees grew along the edge of the lake, and his cabin was slightly around the bend and on a small rise.

The quilt that the Piece Makers had left her was tucked around her, and she was grateful for it, as it was chilly outside. But the place was so peaceful, so calm and serene, she had to be outside, soaking it all in. So different from the noise and smell and impersonal atmosphere of the city.

The city stole her soul while the peaceful scene before her fed it.

She closed her eyes, breathing the chill air deeply. She hadn't even unpacked. Just set her suitcases in the middle of the floor and had practically tripped over the heels of the Piece Makers, four sweet little old ladies, as they had left. She didn't know what their rush was in leaving, but she'd been in a hurry to get out and try out the rocking chair on the front porch.

She'd made a quick trip back inside to grab the quilt, since it was too chilly to be comfortable outside without it.

But after the long drive, after all the stress of making and promoting her latest movie and dealing with all of the rumors of her latest breakup, not to mention the lawyers and her agent, the peace in this place was a necessary balm to her soul.

Every once in a while, the steel blue eyes of the cowboy she'd met on the street shot through her head, which was odd, since she'd seen a lot of handsome men in her life. Kissed many of them and worked with even more.

So it wasn't the man's looks that caused him to stick in her head, no matter the color of his eyes. Or the shape of his nose. Or the angle of his jaw.

It was something else. But she didn't trust herself, not with men, anyway. Her judgment, based on past experience, was terrible.

She knew that to be true, and yet, it didn't explain why her heartbeat kicked up as she saw in the distance what looked like an old beat-up truck coming up over the rise.

Somehow she knew it was him before he even pulled in front of her porch, stopping on the gravel road, waiting while the boy sitting in the passenger seat rolled the window down.

Funny that Rem and Elaine hadn't mentioned children, but there was that one in the passenger seat and then two on the bench seat behind them, surrounded by book bags and duffels.

He didn't seem surprised to see her, and she assumed that he had known immediately after their meeting on the street, where she'd practically run him over, that she was the movie star who would be staying here. It had been a while since she'd been in a small town, but she knew how they worked. Everyone knew everything about everybody.

She, on the other hand, had no idea that the cowboy that she'd met would be the one who would be staying up here.

But why else would anyone be up here in the middle of nowhere, driving around?

"You must be Miss Levine," the cowboy said, with a hint of a smile around the corners of his mouth, although it didn't detract from the serious look on his face.

"I am. You must be the caretaker." She couldn't think of a derogatory word, one that would put him in his place. Other than servant. Which seemed to be going a little bit far.

"Yes, ma'am. If you need anything, I'll be over there in the cabin catty-corner from here. You can hardly see it through the pine trees, but it's not that far to walk if you can't holler."

"You can give me your phone number, and then I won't need to...holler," she said, lifting her nose ever so slightly, telling him clearly that she did not "holler" for anyone.

"I can give you my number, but in my experience, service up here is spotty, more off than on."

She couldn't keep her eyes from widening at that information. She hadn't been here long enough to figure that out. She'd been so enraptured by the view and the peace and the stillness and the way her soul just soaked it all in, needing it, and she hadn't even known.

"Why don't you give it to me anyway?" She didn't think he was the kind of man who would lie. In fact, she figured he was probably the kind of man who couldn't lie, but nonetheless, she pulled her phone out from under her leg, her hands leaving the snuggly warmth of the quilt, and pulled up her contact list, waiting for him to rattle his number off.

He did so, and she typed it in. She did not send him a text though. Somehow, it made her feel like the playing field was more even when she had his number but he didn't have hers. After all, he shouldn't need to get a hold of her. It would just be her needing him.

And maybe she wouldn't.

The sweet ladies from town had taken care of her better than she expected, and what they'd given her, and the groceries she'd bought when she stopped in Sweet Water earlier, would tide her over for a while.

The man waited, as though expecting her to either text him or give him her number in return.

When she did neither, he looked straight ahead, almost trying to figure out what to do since the situation hadn't gone as planned, but his voice was easy and his look mild when he turned back toward her, leaning forward just a bit to see her around the head of the kid in front.

Interesting that the man's eyes were blue and his hair sandy blond, while the kid's eyes were black, his hair dark.

Bellamy didn't dwell on that though, as the man said, "Call or text if you need anything. I'll be at one of the cabins, either working or hanging out with the boys."

"Hmm," she said, making it sound like she wasn't committing to anything. She'd have to really need him, as in a major emergency, before she would voluntarily text him. She wanted to be alone. She wanted to gather herself and heal. She definitely didn't want to be dealing with some man and his three children.

Although she didn't see a wife, she was probably around somewhere too. Funny he didn't mention her.

As she thought that, her eyes drifted over the man's hands, strong and brown, as they gripped the steering wheel. There were no rings. Not on any of the fingers.

The man drove away, and as though seeing him had destroyed the peaceful atmosphere, Bellamy stood, figuring now that twilight had descended, she'd better go in and get acclimated to her new home.

It had been beautifully designed, open and spacious with stainless steel appliances and leather furniture. She hadn't been upstairs, but if the downstairs was any indication, the place would be amazing.

Watching his taillights fade off into the distance, amazed at how quickly dusk descended, she turned, opening the door and stepping into the house.

It was open, with plenty of windows to let in the daylight, but it felt dark and dim now that the sun had gone down.

She reached for the light switch, feeling along the wall, finally touching it with her fingers, flipping on all three switches. Surely one of them would light the kitchen area or the living room.

The porch light came on, and nothing else.

Confused, she flicked the nearest switch again.

Nothing. She flipped it several more times, still nothing. She tried the middle switch and got the exact same result. The far switch turned the porch light on and off.

That was odd.

It wasn't quite so dark that she needed to pull her phone out of her pocket to use the flashlight app to see. The kitchen island loomed gray and dark, and if memory served, there was nothing between her and it, so she walked carefully toward it. Then she felt along the counter, remembering there had been a switch by the sink.

Feeling for it, she breathed a sigh of relief when the kitchen lights turned on above the sink.

Realizing she was thirsty, she flipped the handle to let the water grow cold, planning to open the cupboard and look for a glass.

There was no water.

Her brow scrunched up, and she tried again. Nothing. She moved the faucet up and down and over and back. Not a drop.

Really? I come here to get away from everyone and everything. God, I know I walked away from You. I came here to find my way back. To find what I left.

She grunted.

And this is what You do? You have the things in this house not working so I have no choice but to talk to the man that's stuck in my head? God, You know I've sworn off men. I don't want to need a man to be happy. Don't want to have to have someone constantly telling me I'm beautiful to feel like I'm worth something. I want to feel worth as Your child. So why are You allowing this?

There was no answer.

Determined that she wouldn't allow this to ruin her evening, she decided that whatever needed to be fixed, she'd make a list and talk to the man in the morning. Unless she couldn't take a shower. That was something she definitely needed tonight.

She should probably find out his name. If there were lights and water lines that both needed to be fixed, they probably were going to be having a lot more contact than what she had originally anticipated.

Lord, I hope You know what You're doing.

Chapter 8

Being faithful and true to your spouse and putting God first.
- Ann from Cleveland, MS

"I want my mommy." Cayson stuck his thumb in his mouth and stared up at Calhoun. As soon as the idea of going to bed had been presented, Cayson had gone from precocious and happy to pretty much melting into a sobbing mess.

Calvin had told Calhoun that Cayson was seven. Calhoun wasn't sure at what age kids usually stopped sucking their thumbs, but he thought it was maybe younger than that.

Regardless, he'd stood in front of the judge and told her he'd do his very best to take care of the children when she granted him guardianship, not that he wouldn't do his very best even if he hadn't promised, but he was feeling like a failure right now.

"Sorry, buddy." He wasn't sure what else to say, but the little boy didn't resist when Calhoun wrapped his arms around him and picked him up.

It had been a big day for everyone, and the kid was obviously tired, laying his head down and sobbing softly into Calhoun's neck.

The other two boys stared at him with wide, sad eyes, and Calhoun said a silent prayer that they wouldn't dissolve into tears too.

He'd been scared about the whole reading thing, but he hadn't banked on tears. He wasn't good with emotions of any stripe, but tears were his least favorite.

"Are you guys going to start leaking on me too?" he asked with a lifted brow, phrasing it in a way that he hoped would get a laugh out of them. It worked, as their mouths both turned up and they shook their heads.

"I didn't realize it was going to take so long in Rockerton today, but I don't have your beds ready. We'll fix that tomorrow. Do you think you can sleep in the bunk beds, or do we need to spread out a sleeping bag on the floor?" He needed to order a mattress as well. He hadn't thought of it, and he shoved aside the voice that wanted to tell him he wasn't cut out to be a dad or to have guardianship of these boys.

"I can share a bed with Cayson," Calvin said. "We're used to it. We always sleep together." He looked over at Cruz, nodding. "Sometimes he sleeps with us, too."

"At the last house, there was only one bed for the three of us. Sometimes I hated it because Cayson kicks in his sleep, but sometimes when I'm scared, it's nice to have my brothers beside me." Cruz, who Calhoun had already figured out was the most serious of the boys, spoke without much emotion.

"All right then. You guys can grab your toothbrushes out of your bags and brush your teeth, and I'll see what I can do for your brother."

"We don't have toothbrushes." Calvin looked scared, like that knowledge was going to be the thing that finally made Calhoun mad. All day, it had kinda seemed like they were waiting for him to get angry. He figured that they were probably used to living with adults who yelled at them since that's what they seemed to be waiting for.

"It sounds like we're going to have to make a list of the things we need to get. Mattress. Toothbrush. I suppose we need to put toothpaste on the list as well?"

The boys nodded.

Calhoun grinned. "I wonder if we can find a store that sells both mattresses and toothpaste?"

"We were in a store once that had everything. At least that's what Mom said," Calvin offered helpfully. Then his little thin shoulders shrugged. "But I can't remember what the name of it was."

Calhoun grunted, his hand gently patting the back of the boy who was no longer sobbing in his arms. In fact, his breathing had evened out. Calhoun wouldn't have been the slightest bit surprised to find out that he was sleeping. He didn't ask the boys whether or not his eyes were closed. It was probably too soon for the boy to be in a deep enough sleep that being talked about wouldn't wake him up.

"Whatever the name was, I'm pretty sure it wasn't located in Sweet Water. We might have to do some traveling tomorrow."

"Those ladies we talked to in town said they'd do anything for you that you wanted them to," Cruz said, looking up from where he had just picked up his book bag.

Calhoun nodded, remembering the Piece Makers had practically fallen over themselves to offer to help them out. He hated to ask people to do things for him. He liked to be the person who served others, not the one who needed help. But maybe this was an exception in his life. It wasn't every day that a single man became the guardian to three boys overnight. He supposed it was acceptable for him to need some help.

"I bet they could provide us with a quilt for the bed, and I bet my brothers would get us a mattress. So all we'll need to do is make the bed."

"You mean like...build it ourselves?" Calvin asked, half awed, half eager.

Calhoun nodded. "That's kinda what I do. I build things." What he did on the side anyway. His family was a trucking family, and building things wasn't exactly at a premium there. But working with wood was his first love.

No point in explaining all that to the boys.

"I want to build things too. Can I sleep in the bed we make?" Cruz asked.

"No! I get to. I'm the oldest," Calvin insisted.

Calhoun wanted to step in before it became a full-blown argument and they woke up Cayson, or at least reminded him that he wasn't crying, but before he could, his phone dinged from his pocket.

"Do you guys have jammies?" he asked as he pulled his phone out with one hand, carefully holding Cayson still in his position with the other.

"Not really. Mom usually makes us put clean clothes on before we go to bed, but not always," Calvin said with a shrug.

"We'll have to do that then. Throw your old clothes on the floor for now. I'll put a clothes hamper on our list of things we need to get." The list of things that kept getting longer and longer the more they stood here and talked. All these crazy obvious things he hadn't thought of.

"You do that while I answer this," he said, indicating his phone.

The boys nodded and opened up their book bags.

He looked down at his phone and almost didn't answer because he didn't recognize the number. It could be one of their company's drivers having a problem, although he wasn't the one who usually took those calls. Still, it might have to do with the trucking company somehow because of the late hour, so he swiped and put it to his ear.

"Hello?"

"Are you the person who's supposed to be helping me if I need something?" a cultured voice asked from the other end of the line.

The same cultured voice that had caused the hair on the back of his neck to stand up that morning when she spoke to him from the driver's seat of her sports car.

It was the fancy actress.

"I don't know. What's your name?" He didn't know why he was being so difficult. Other than he really couldn't remember her first name. Although he suspected he was the only man in America who didn't know it

"Very funny, cowboy. I was trying to be nice. I wasn't going to call until tomorrow morning, but I don't have any water."

Calhoun closed his eyes and leaned his head back. How could she not have any water? He'd done all the plumbing himself. And while he hadn't checked it earlier today, everything had been working fine when he'd finished and told Rem it was ready.

"Did you try every spigot?" he asked, unsure of what else to say.

"I don't know. The lights aren't working either. I could live without them. But I can't not take a shower."

"Of course not. We wouldn't want you to go to bed without a shower." He couldn't keep the sarcasm out of his voice. He'd gone to bed plenty of times with no shower, too exhausted to stand up. But usually that was about seven o'clock in the morning after he'd worked all night. And all day the day before.

He doubted the fancy actress had any idea that people might put those kinds of hours into a workday.

God resists the proud but gives grace to the humble.

Yeah. His thoughts were sarcastic, which equaled proud. He wanted to put the actress down, knock her off her pedestal so they were on the same footing. He didn't know why that was so important to him. Humility wasn't usually something that he struggled with quite this much. But there it was. He didn't want to have to look up to the actress.

"I guess I could call Mr. Martinez. And while I'm at it, I suppose I could tell him that the person he left to take care of me isn't doing a very good job." There was haughtiness in her tone, and it convicted Calhoun all over again of the pride in his own. She obviously didn't want him to have the upper hand and wanted to put herself above him as well.

They could either fight like this, or he could do what he knew he should and just be humble.

It grated, but he cleared his throat and said, "I'm sorry. You're right. It's my job to make sure you have water and electricity. I'm not sure exactly what the problem could be, but I'll come right over...well..."

He couldn't explain about the boys. Not to this actress. She wouldn't understand about common people problems.

"It's going to be about twenty minutes until I can make it over." He forced his voice not to sound arrogant but humble.

"Of course. I wouldn't want you to have to turn the TV off and miss the rest of your show just because I'm sitting over here without water and electricity."

His jaw muscles bunched, but he kept his teeth firmly planted together. She was frustrated because she didn't have lights and she didn't have water. He would be the same. Especially if he didn't know how to fix it.

Also, he thought as he looked over at the boys and rubbed his hand over the back of the boy lying over his shoulder, maybe she was scared too. The big-city actress probably wasn't used to being out in the country with no other humans, aside from what she probably considered an incompetent cowboy, within yelling distance.

Maybe that was the reason she called more than the fact that she didn't have lights or water. Although if she were scared, that probably made the other problems worse. More like a horror movie, not that Calhoun had ever watched any. But a man could assume probably somewhere in a horror movie the lights went out at least. The water probably wasn't quite as big of a buildup.

With those thoughts, he did something he wouldn't normally do, and he explained himself. "I have three young boys here who just had their mother leave them today, and they're staying with me for the first time. I need to get them settled before I can walk away from them. I don't know how long it's going to take to fix your problems, and I don't want to head over there until I know they're gonna be okay here."

There was silence on the other end of the line. Maybe she did have a heart. Maybe his thoughts were wrong, and he'd been thinking of her as a stuck-up snobby actress instead of giving her the benefit of the doubt and assuming the best of her instead of the worst.

"I didn't realize the children you had with you were with you for the first time." Her voice kind of dropped off like she wanted to ask questions about that. He supposed that was natural. She was probably wondering if he was the father. He would be wondering the same thing if it were one of his brothers.

But he'd already said more than what he normally would have and didn't offer any more information.

Although a thought struck him, and he spoke without thinking. "If you really want to have a shower right now, the electricity and water are both working in my cabin. You're welcome to come over and help yourself."

"No—" Her no cut off like she had said it without thinking. "Actually..." Her voice trailed off.

He waited, wondering if she were fighting herself because she didn't want to come to his cabin, or if there was something else.

And then he realized that maybe she was afraid to walk through the dark night.

"I know it's pretty isolated and maybe a little more rugged than what you're used to. I can step outside and keep an eye on you if you're driving over."

"Don't be silly. I'm a grown woman. I don't need to be babysat to go a hundred yards." Her voice held snob, but then, as though all the arrogance had deflated out of her, she said, "I'm sorry. I don't know why I got so defensive when you hit the nail right on the head. I... I've never been somewhere so desolate."

"Maybe you'll get used to it. Most of us who live here love it that way." He wouldn't change it for the world. But he could understand how it might be scary to someone like her. He supposed if he went to the city, he would be uncomfortable with all the lights and noise and people. Funny how a person acclimated to what they lived in, and everything else seemed foreign and uncomfortable.

The city might not be scary to him exactly, but it would probably be overwhelming.

"Hardly. I won't be here that long."

"I'd be careful if I were you. North Dakota has a way of making you fall in love with her." He said that with a little bit of humor in his voice, but he meant it with all his heart. He loved his state, the wide openness, the big sky, even the unrelenting wind, with a fierceness and ferocity that he couldn't even explain.

But the woman snorted. "I wouldn't bet on that." Then, almost under her breath, she said, "I'm done falling in love."

Her words reminded him that she'd been going through a hard time. A divorce, nasty and hard, the way divorces often were, and very public, because of her job.

Pity swept through him, a feeling she probably wouldn't welcome. He refused to allow it in his voice when he said, "So does that mean you're coming over or not?"

"I think I better stay put. You seem kind of eager to have me there, and I suppose I learned a long time ago that I need to be careful."

Her voice was still cultured, but it had lost some of the haughtiness, and he didn't take offense. He supposed she had a lot of fans, a lot of men, who wanted more from her than she wanted to give.

Probably there were some who had a hard time taking no for an answer.

"I don't blame you for being cautious," he said sincerely.

He looked around. The boys had long since disappeared, and he figured they were probably changed for the night. Cayson was a dead weight on his shoulder, and while he could feel the wet, cold spot where his tears had soaked his T-shirt, he thought the boy was asleep, and those little noises were probably snores.

"I don't think it will take long to put the boys to bed. They're tired. Then I'll be right over."

"I'll be waiting. Dirty and in the dark. Take your time." Then, like she'd done twice before, she seemed to deflate, and she said, "Sorry. Take care of the children first. I'm a grown woman. I can wait."

"You're a grown woman, but you're still in a strange place, a place that can be scary before you fall in love with it." He couldn't help adding that, teasing her a little, maybe because he wanted her to smile, or maybe because he just wanted to needle her. He wasn't sure.

"I assume you're still talking about the state of North Dakota and not with any cowboys who might be wandering around the area."

"I should be the only cowboy wandering around the area, and it might be a stretch to call me a cowboy. Despite the hat."

"What? You don't own a horse or a cow? I thought everyone out here owned cows or chased them or worshipped them or something."

He laughed, even though she wasn't exactly being complimentary. "No. I don't own any cows. I might someday, but the only thing I really do with cows right now is eat them."

She gasped, kinda outraged maybe, and he wondered vaguely if she might be a vegetarian. He might have offended her. And he hadn't even meant to.

Then she laughed. "I guess we have that in common."

He chuckled. "Well, that was an accident. Finding we have something in common."

"It sure is. I would have sworn that we had absolutely nothing in common."

"Better be careful, or we'll find more. Including being in love with North Dakota." Calhoun couldn't let that go. If it were a horse, it would have been beaten to death a long time ago.

"I can guarantee you we will never have that in common. I'm a city girl, and it's true that maybe I wanted to get away for a little bit, but I will never love this empty desolate godforsaken place. Does the wind ever quit blowing?" she asked in exaggerated exasperation.

"Not very often. When it does, you better look out. It's always the calm before the storm."

"Thanks for the warning. I guess I should stop wishing it stops then, right?"

"Yeah. Pretty much."

She sighed. Funny that she didn't seem to be in any bigger rush to get off the phone than he was. "I'll let you put your boys to bed. I'll see you before midnight?"

He didn't know what time it was, but he agreed. It shouldn't take long to put the boys down. "Before midnight for sure. Hopefully you'll have a shower and be in bed by then."

"If that happens, I'll call you a miracle worker instead of a cowboy, Cowboy."

"Hang tight. I'll be there." He didn't wait for her to say anything else but slid his phone off, shaking his head and shoving it back in his pocket.

He hadn't wanted to like the lady. He wanted to think of her as a princess, too good for everyone else, but the reality was she was human and just as broken as everyone else. Maybe even more so, because everything hurt worse when it happened in the spotlight.

When someone had a lot, he supposed it was human tendency to expect a lot out of them, but just because someone was rich didn't make them any stronger than anyone else.

He shifted Cayson on his shoulder and dragged his mind back to the task at hand: these boys that he promised to take care of. He needed to focus on them first. Get them settled, make sure they were okay.

He debated about whether or not he should tell Calvin that he was leaving, since he didn't really know the kid. Maybe he would try to get away with something while Calhoun was gone, but he kinda thought it would be better that if one of the boys woke up, at least Calvin would know why he might not be there, and they wouldn't panic.

Deciding it was best to be honest and to trust the boy until he proved himself untrustworthy, Calhoun turned and went toward the bedroom with the littlest one still over his shoulder and with his heart feeling bigger than usual. Maybe, along with the love of his home state, there would be enough room in his heart to love three little boys.

And a movie star.

He wasn't sure where that thought came from, but as much as he wanted to reject it out of hand, because he didn't want to be one of her many millions of admirers, he found he couldn't.

Chapter 9

Being best friends.
– Heather from Canada

Bellamy sat in the kitchen under the only light in the entire downstairs that worked.

Upstairs, there were two bedrooms and two baths. The light in one bathroom worked, but there wasn't a single faucet in the entire cabin that worked.

She figured there was a control panel somewhere, and maybe all that was needed to fix the lights was for a fuse to be flipped or something—she wasn't even sure of the correct terminology, just that it might be an easy fix. She hoped, anyway.

She was trying to be patient.

The man had said twenty minutes, but it had been at least twice that long since they'd hung up.

Finally, a knock at her door startled her. She hadn't heard a motor or seen lights. Not that she could have heard anything over the howling wind.

She jumped up, took a breath to settle herself, and tried to walk regally to the door, although she supposed she probably practically ran.

Throwing it open, she had to bite her tongue not to berate the man. But she couldn't keep one caustic comment from coming out. "I thought you were going to wait until morning."

The man seemed calm, quiet, and blessedly not arrogant. She hated dealing with arrogant people, and they were everywhere in LA. At least around her anyway.

"Sorry. I told you about the boys. I was holding one while I was talking to you, and he woke up when I laid him down. He cried for a while, and I couldn't leave him."

The man spoke, then didn't wait for her to invite him in, but stepped in, looking around. He closed the door as his free hand went to the light switches, like he knew exactly where they were, and flipped each one, noting as she had that two didn't work. Then noting the porch light that flipped off and then back on.

"Interesting. It won't be a fuse that's blown since one of the three still work. Still, I'll check the breaker box." He moved toward the door in the kitchen which she had assumed to be a pantry but turned out to be stairs to the cellar. He went down them, disappearing into the darkness after trying to flip the light and it didn't work.

She heard some banging around, saw the glow and bob of what she assumed was his cell phone flashlight. She sat down at the bar, waiting, and about five minutes later, he came back up the stairs.

"Well. I can hardly believe it because this just never happens around Sweet Water, but someone has broken in and tampered with some things. A lot of the fuses were switched off, but I think it was mostly because they switched them off before they started cutting wires. They missed a couple, which explains why you have some lights but not a lot."

A muscle ticked in and out of his jaw, which Bellamy assumed meant that he was upset, although there was no other outward sign. "It feels random, like it was done in a hurry. And I assume it was someone who knew what they were doing. Anyway, you're not going to have lights or water tonight. The water was shut off, but I didn't turn it back on because a large section of pipe along the wall in the basement is completely cut out."

The whole time he'd been talking, his eyes were going around the kitchen, seeming to touch on everything, the curtains, the stainless steel appliances, the gift baskets, the string that had tied the quilt together that she hadn't thrown away, and even the wall art.

Then his eyes flicked back to the gift baskets.

He walked slowly over to where she sat at the bar in front of the basket that held bath salts and an assortment of shower gels and shampoos.

He touched something in the basket.

"What doesn't belong?" he said with a grunt.

She looked at his fingers which were touching the blade of some kind of saw with a handle on it.

"I didn't even notice that in there."

"Kind of looks like whoever did this was trying to hide what they were doing by shoving the blade in this basket and never remembered to take it back out."

Bellamy thought back to when she had walked into the cabin for the first time. The Piece Makers, such sweet, darling ladies, the kind of ladies that made a small town feel like home and made her feel so welcomed and loved, had been standing in the kitchen, as though they were talking amongst themselves.

Now that she thought about it, there maybe had been a furtive glance or two and some odd movement as well.

But that was probably just her cynical nature being suspicious of everyone in hindsight. Those ladies were so sweet and innocent, they would never have done anything like this.

But they were the ones who left the basket.

Odd that the saw would be in the basket, and the quilting ladies were the last ones here.

"The Piece Makers is the quilting group in Sweet Water?"

The man nodded his head like he knew who she was talking about.

So she continued. "They were the ones who left the baskets. And they were here when I walked in."

"They were here?" he said immediately.

"Yes. Standing in the kitchen talking. That said, they brought the welcome baskets, and they put some flowers in my bedroom. They also left an arrangement of teas and coffees and another one of some grocery items. And a quilt that I left out on the porch on the rocking chair. It was all very sweet and thoughtful."

He had nodded at everything she talked about. And then she said, "They were such lovely ladies. Someone might have taken advantage of them somehow, but I can't imagine how they could have done that, gotten a saw put in their basket. There was only one car here."

It was all very confusing, but maybe that was because she was so tired.

Or maybe it was because of the presence of the cowboy in front of her. It wasn't that he was so much bigger than any man she'd ever seen, because he wasn't. But he seemed serious and honest. He almost oozed character and integrity and competence, and she wasn't used to it.

He gave her the impression that it didn't matter what happened, he would do the right thing, no matter what it cost him. Maybe that was just fanciful thinking on her part. Maybe she watched too many westerns as a child and saw the white hat as the good boy always doing right. She'd let her creative imagination take over.

The man didn't say anything, just stood there, although the look on his face said he had some suspicions.

"You know. I guess I should have introduced myself. I'm sorry I was a little sarcastic on the phone." She pushed out of her chair and held her hand over the island countertop. "I'm Bellamy Levine."

He looked at her hand for a minute, almost as though trying to shift gears from what he'd been thinking that had furrowed his brow and focus on what she had just said.

She was almost ready to take her hand back when his own hand, bigger and rougher than hers, came out and clasped hers with what she felt was a very ginger and delicate grip. Almost as though he was afraid he would hurt her.

"Calhoun."

"It's good to meet you, Calhoun. I promise I really don't want to be a pain."

She had the feeling he was trying not to roll his eyes. She thought about all the changes that her assistant had demanded. She had vaguely known about them but had not tried to stop them just because she had so much other garbage going on in her life.

He probably had certain ideas about her, because more than likely he was the one who had been tasked with making those changes.

He probably had felt like the work that he had done hadn't been good enough. That *she* had felt like his work wasn't good enough.

If that were true, it was a wonder he was even talking to her.

Feeling like she should apologize but not sure how to approach the subject, because after all, she was making assumptions, and she could be completely wrong, she just said, "It's nice to meet you. I'm sorry we didn't get off on the right foot very well. Obviously it's not your fault that my water and lights aren't working."

"No. But it's my job to make sure they do. I told you that I would be over here fixing them tonight, but this isn't a job that I'm going to get done tonight."

He hesitated, looking down. "This actually might not be a job that I'm going to be able to do this week. I'm missing some specialized joints, ones that will have to be ordered in." He looked up at her, uncertainty on his face. "I really am not trying to take advantage of you in any way, but my cabin is the only cabin that has lights and electricity and running water. I would offer to trade you cabins, but I told you about the three boys I have. I... I think they would probably be pretty happy roughing it over here, but I... I'm new at this whole...dad...thing. For lack of a better word."

"So you're new at being a dad. It's okay." She had to admit she was curious why this man had never been a father to his children. He didn't seem like the type who would walk away from his responsibilities. But obviously that's what he'd done.

"Well. There's a little more to it than that. It's late. I can... I can stay here if you want to use my cabin. But...the boys are my responsibility."

"I'm sorry. I know you're not trying to pull anything. I've learned to be suspicious of people. I suppose because people have done things to me in the past, but I'm sorry that made me accuse you of things that you're not responsible for."

She wasn't offering a very good apology at all, but she didn't know how else to say it. She'd been unkind to him. And he didn't deserve her suspicion. He was just trying to be nice.

"Well, thanks. I guess I'm also thinking that whoever did this could possibly be back. Although I highly doubt it. I'm going to need to talk to Rem some tomorrow. It just seems like they were vandalizing things for the sake of vandalizing them. Not to steal anything. Because I don't notice anything missing. At the very least, they could have taken the hundred-dollar blender that's sitting on the countertop. But they didn't."

"Is that how much the blender cost?"

His brows lifted as he nodded, but then they relaxed and he smiled a little, seeming to laugh at himself, and she felt stupid. Because obviously he was thinking she was a spoiled rich movie star who didn't shop at the stores that the rest of the world shopped at.

And he was kind of right.

It had been a long time since she'd been to an actual store. That's what her assistant was for. She had gone shopping for clothing, but normal people didn't shop on Rodeo Drive.

Thoughts of her assistant turned her stomach, and she placed a hand over it.

Letting it go for now, not wanting to get sucked into that hole again, she weighed her options. She could insist on staying at her cabin with no electricity and water. She could insist that he stay here with no electricity and no water with or without the boys. She supposed she could take responsibility for the three boys, maybe, or they could go back over to his cabin together.

"How many bedrooms are in your cabin?"

"Just two. The boys are using one. You can have the other. And the other bathroom. I'll sleep on the couch."

"I don't want to put you out of your room," she said automatically, although she meant it. She wasn't here to cause problems. She was here to fix her own problems. Or at least to give herself some space to heal. This was the last thing she needed.

Lord, I came here to find You. Instead, You dumped a whole new set of problems in my lap. Why can't You quit picking on me and pick on someone else?

But even as she thought that, she knew that God had a plan for her life. Apparently this cowboy and his three children were part of it.

"You're not putting me out. I'll be fine. I guess if I want to get my room back, I can work harder and faster on fixing your cabin up for you."

"That makes sense." It was late, and she wasn't going to overthink this. "Let me grab my stuff. It's all here. I didn't even take it upstairs, and I'll come with you."

"I walked over. I didn't want the boys to get up and look out and not see my truck beside the cabin and get scared. Do you mind walking back? Because I can run over and grab it as long as I'm coming right back."

"No. It's fine. As long as you're here, and it's not that far." Surprisingly, she felt like she was making the right decision as she gathered her stuff, then followed the imposing cowboy out into the dark North Dakota night.

Chapter 10

When you get upset with your partner, think about it. Is it going to matter in one week? No? Let it go! Is it going to matter in one month? No? Let it go! Too often we get so caught up in being offended that we blow the offense out of proportion.
- Maria McGee from Georgia

"Where's the rest of your math books?" Calhoun asked, working hard to keep the astonishment and irritation out of his voice as he fingered one small notebook.

Calvin blinked up at him. Despite the fact that Calhoun thought he'd done a good job of keeping his emotions in check, Calvin still looked like he was shrinking in on himself. Maybe he knew, without anyone having to tell him, that the schooling his mother had been doing with him was not nearly enough.

"That's it."

"So did you do something like this last year too?" Calhoun asked, hoping that maybe she just hadn't gotten the books purchased for this year yet.

"That is my notebook from last year."

Well, it was no wonder the other two couldn't read. The wonder was actually that Calvin could, since the reading material they were using was even more sparse than the math. Calvin had told him that their reading books consisted of library books. Which was fine. Calhoun's mom, and then his dad, had done the same thing with their homeschooling. The only problem was these boys hadn't been in one place long enough to actually get a library card and use the library.

"All right. We'll get a few more things to supplement this, and you'll be good to go."

He glanced at the younger boys, whose math and reading and other subjects weren't any better than Calvin's. Worse actually. But he already set them to working on a few easy problems in the few books they had.

He looked at the list he had made as they'd gone through their stuff. He basically needed entire curriculums for all three boys.

He'd never priced homeschool material, but he couldn't imagine it would be cheap. But the price really wasn't an object. What he was wondering was whether he was even qualified to be doing this on his own, or whether he should just throw in the towel and call child services. Maybe a school would handle them better.

Maybe a school would be worse.

True. Since he had a personal interest in the boys, not because any of them were his, but just because they were here in front of him, and he could give them one-on-one time daily.

"Whether you think you can, or you think you can't – you're right," Henry Ford's quote came into his head.

It was all about attitude. Attitude and hard work.

He knew he could do the work, and he figured he could control his attitude as well.

Still, it was scary to have the futures of three humans entirely in his hands. It seemed arrogant of him to assume that he could do it.

Scribbling down "check into North Dakota homeschool laws," he had reached for the next book in the stack on the table when a shadow fell and the hair on his arms pricked.

He knew without looking up that it was Bellamy.

"Good morning, boys." Bellamy's voice hadn't gotten any less appealing to him overnight. He'd never heard a voice that sounded sultry and innocent at the same time. If her acting skills were even a tiny fraction as good as her voice, it was no wonder she was America's favorite actress.

And it was no wonder she had been married five times either.

Apparently her ability to *stay* married wasn't quite as good as her ability to *get* married.

Calhoun tried to push both of those thoughts aside, since neither one of them was anything he wanted to dwell on. He didn't want to care about Bellamy's personal life.

The boys looked up when she spoke. Cruz shrank back in his chair a little. Calvin seemed interested, and Cayson, totally forgetting his tears of the night before, grinned and said, "You're pretty!"

That wasn't quite what Calhoun was thinking. Beautiful was more like it.

He'd seen plenty of beautiful women with no character underneath the pretty outer shell, and so while his eyes enjoyed the sight, he tried hard to make sure the rest of him was reminded that beauty was only skin-deep.

"Well, thank you. That's a great way to greet a lady in the morning." Bellamy smiled gently. She'd known he had children here, and he hadn't corrected her seeming assumption that they were his. He wasn't sure what to say about it anyway. He wanted them to be and was fighting for it. So it was kind of silly to correct people when they thought they actually were.

"I'm Bellamy. What's your name?" Bellamy stopped beside Cayson's chair with her hand out.

Her hair shone as it fell over her shoulders, and her eyes were bright and cheerful. Her smile was camera perfect, unsurprisingly.

Calhoun turned his eyes away deliberately.

"I'm Cayson, and this is my brother Cruz and my brother Calvin. We live here now."

"I figured you did. Considering that your dad is here too," Bellamy said as she shook his hand seriously.

"He's not our dad. He just wanted us, so Mom gave us away." Cayson's words were simple, childlike, and they made Calhoun's stomach twist hard and ugly.

He didn't want to think about how a mother could give her children away. And how a child could just think that she could and feel like it was normal.

His words had made Bellamy's brows raise, and she slanted a glance at Calhoun, even as she turned to Cruz and held her hand out. He gazed at her, distrust evident in his eyes.

Calhoun recognized that look too. The look that said *I loved my mom, and she gave me away, so I don't trust any woman.*

Calhoun could totally relate to that sentiment. He'd gone through that on his own. Maybe it had ended up being a good thing, because it made him go to God and tell the Lord that he would wait for the right woman and trust God to bring her along since he couldn't trust himself to find her on his own.

God had sure been taking His sweet time with it, considering that had been fifteen years ago, and God hadn't brought anyone that was even close to what Calhoun was expecting.

Maybe Bellamy is the one.

Hardly. She'd been married five times. And she was a movie star. And she was beautiful. And when she left North Dakota, she would never be back.

At the very least, I want someone who loves where I live. I'm not leaving North Dakota. Not for a woman.

Maybe he was being too picky, but the idea that Bellamy was the one for him was ridiculous. He wasn't going to argue about it anymore.

Bellamy had smiled at Cruz, and he had shaken her hand, very reluctantly. Calvin was a little more forthcoming, although his look was more derisive. Calhoun could understand that as well.

"I made the boys pancakes for breakfast. There are two on that plate underneath the lid. If you want to eat them, they're yours," Calhoun said, forcing his fingers to pick up the next book even though his eyes didn't really see it. He figured she wouldn't eat pancakes, because they probably had some kind of ingredient that didn't mesh with her diet.

To his surprise, she nodded and asked the boys if they were good. When they all nodded their heads eagerly, she grinned, saying she would give them a try, and walked over to the stove, her movements graceful, her limbs long and slender.

Calhoun found himself staring and again had to tear his eyes away.

Maybe, instead of thinking that the boys' schooling was the most important thing, he should have gone straight over to her cabin and started working on it so he could get it fixed so she could get out of his.

He made a mental note as he lifted the book in his hand: the next thing on his list would be fixing Bellamy's cabin.

"I'm gonna need to run into town today. I have some things I need to get for the boys, including some snow clothes and things for outside." They didn't have a stitch of winter clothes beyond hooded sweatshirts. Calhoun couldn't suppress the feeling that the boys were better off without their mother, even if it was wrong. "I also have to make an order of the things I need to fix your cabin and pick up what I can at the hardware store. If you need anything, you're welcome to ride along or give me a list and I'll do my best with it." He hoped she would just give him a list. He didn't really want to ride into town with her.

"That sounds wonderful. I'll ride along. In fact, if we're going over lunch, I'll treat you all to lunch on me at the diner in town. It looked like a nice place."

Calhoun had his mouth open to decline her offer—the very last thing he wanted was to be stuck at a table across from her in public—when he noticed that the boys were all sitting in their chairs looking eager.

Cayson said, "We ate there yesterday! It was awesome! I had a hot dog. It was the best hot dog I've ever had in my entire life! And they made the fries in the shape of a smiley face! And I got all the ketchup I wanted."

"That pretty much makes it the best diner ever," Bellamy said with a grin that matched Cayson's.

He didn't want her to get along with the boys. He didn't want them to do things together. This was just a temporary arrangement until he could get her out of their cabin and back into her own.

He was thinking about that a little later as he stood with his hands on his hips in the basement looking again at the sawed-off pipes.

Someone had known what they were doing. They'd shut the water off and cut the pipes that would be the most damaging. They'd also taken out his joints, and the last time he'd ordered the parts he would need, they'd been back-ordered. "Supply chain issues" is what Jenson at the hardware store had said. He couldn't imagine that the supply chain issues had gotten any better, since nothing else had.

If he recalled correctly, it had taken eight to ten weeks in order to get the parts in.

Eight to ten weeks. The thought made him almost physically ill.

"Did you get lost down there?" Bellamy's voice came floating down the stairs. He could hear the boys' footsteps above. She had offered to watch them while he went down and made a list of the things he needed.

"Nah," he said, like it was a legitimate question and not rhetorical. He couldn't bring any other words to his tongue at that moment though. He supposed he and Bellamy needed to have a major talk.

He'd spoken with Rem a little on the phone the night before after he'd gotten Bellamy settled upstairs in the bedroom with the attached bath and told her that she could have the entire upstairs, which included both bedrooms, the bath, and a small area that overlooked the cathedral ceiling downstairs, while he would stay downstairs with the boys so she'd have some privacy.

He'd hoped it was only going to be for a few days.

He'd told Rem that much as well. Rem had sounded tired, and Calhoun could hear children in the background, even though it was late, so he kept the call brief, assuring Rem that he would take care of whatever needed to be dealt with.

Rem had trusted him completely and told him to send the bills to him, and he would make sure that Calhoun was reimbursed.

He declined when Calhoun had asked if he wanted to have the police involved and to try prosecuting.

Rem had said it sounded like someone just messing around, and he told Calhoun that a dog might help keep people away.

It was often the way they did things out where they were. The police weren't going to catch whoever did it, and since nothing was stolen, it was most likely not someone hurting anything. Rem would be out the money for parts, but not for labor, since Calhoun had said he'd do the repairs at no charge, but it wasn't something he was going to get upset over.

Calhoun had been grateful he hadn't had to file a police report but also concerned that it might happen again. Rem had said that if it did, the police should definitely get involved at that point. He said to keep notes on what was missing this time, just so they'd have them for the next.

Rem had remained singularly unconcerned, particularly since nothing had been stolen.

While Calhoun agreed completely with Rem's assessment, he wouldn't have made that decision without Rem's okay, since the property wasn't his.

At least they were on the same page.

He walked slowly back up the stairs, wondering what he was going to tell Bellamy. Wondering how his life had gone from the carefree idea of finishing up cabins over the holidays, enjoying himself, to being responsible for three boys, their schooling, and their entire wardrobes, and now living with a movie star, which seemed a little surreal, since she seemed so down-to-earth. Not that he really knew her.

On top of that, he was supposed to get a dog.

At least the boys would love the dog.

He guessed Bellamy not so much. But she'd have no choice but to stay in the cabin when he brought a dog into it. And if he could find one, he was going to, since, while he didn't feel like there was any danger from what had happened in her cabin, he preferred to have an animal around, just to give them an extra set of eyes and ears.

Technically a nose and ears, since a dog's eyes probably weren't going to be any good.

Grabbing the notebook out of his pocket, he scribbled "dog" down at the end of a very long list, three pages in.

Reaching the top of the stairs, he closed the cellar door behind him and met Bellamy's concerned gaze.

"Is it that bad?" she asked, her forehead wrinkled at the look on his face.

The boys all stood at the window pointing at the snow flurries that were coming down, talking excitedly amongst themselves.

Pulling the notebook back out of his pocket, he put sleds for all three boys below the line that held "dog" on it.

He shoved the notebook back in his pocket. He didn't have to ask the boys if they had sleds. Everything they owned had been in the book bags and duffels that they brought, along with a couple plastic department store bags that mostly held snacks and a random hairbrush. There had been old, broken crayons, a couple of notebooks that apparently doubled as school textbooks, and an alarm clock. That had pretty much rounded out everything the boys owned.

He straightened and took a breath before he answered Bellamy.

"I don't know. I won't until we get to town. But the last time I needed the parts that I'm going to need in order to fix this, they were on back order eight to ten weeks. I can't imagine it's gotten better, but I'm hoping."

"Eight to ten weeks?" she asked, shock and surprise and something that sounded very much like horror in her voice.

He nodded. No point in sugarcoating it. There really wasn't anything to sugarcoat it with.

"I talked to Rem last night. He said you could have your money back if you wanted it. There's nothing we can do to make the repairs go faster. Although last night, I told him it would only take me about four days, which is true once I get the parts. But," he held up his hands, "I can't work with what I don't have."

"I understand." She said that almost like she was offended that he was insulting her intelligence by insinuating that she expected him to pull equipment out of thin air. He hadn't meant it that way, but he figured some people were just easily offended.

Then he remembered their phone conversation. Where she seemed to take his words one way and then realize he probably didn't mean them that way.

As though on cue, she closed her eyes, took a breath, and seemed to force a smile on her face. "I'm sorry. I know you'll do the best you can. You just surprised me, that's all."

"Yeah. I guess I'm not surprised because I ran into some issues when I was putting it together the first time and then when making some of the many corrections that you sent along."

"My assistant sent the corrections."

He paused, his mouth open. It was almost like she was blaming her assistant for the corrections she had wanted done. He wasn't quite sure what to say about that. After all, her assistant wouldn't have made things up on her own.

She shook her head and mumbled, "Never mind."

"All right. It doesn't matter. We might as well head to town now. We'll find out when we get to the store how long it's going to take to get parts in. Last time I asked, Jenson was kind enough to call all the different hardware stores around the area to see if anyone else had any. Maybe someone else has gotten some parts in since last time he checked."

"We can only hope," Bellamy breathed. And then her smile brightened. "I'm sorry. It's not that I'm in a big rush to move out. I just assume I'm probably cramping your space, especially since you're the one sleeping on the couch, and you seem to have so much going on with the boys and everything." She left that open-ended, almost like a question. Like she wanted him to fill in some details about the boys.

If they were going to be living together for two months, maybe he would have to, but not right now.

"Don't worry about it for my sake. Sleeping on the couch is better than sleeping on the floor, but I've done both and neither one bothers me. I prefer indoor plumbing, but beyond that, I could even do without the electricity. Although, it is nice, especially in North Dakota this time of year."

Her mouth opened, closed, then opened again, and she leaned a little closer, almost as though she were confiding something. "Exactly how cold does it get here?"

He found that an odd question.

"You didn't research the climate before you came?" It was as easy as looking on her iPhone. Surely she had a whole boatload of electronics that would tell her what the average temperature was every day from now until doomsday or wherever she wanted from any spot on earth.

"No. I just wanted to get away." She looked down, her words soft and sad, and he remembered the rumors he'd heard about the last movie she made and her ugly divorce. "And now I'm a little afraid."

Her eyes lifted back up, and she seemed to force a smile, although they twinkled too. "Everyone keeps insinuating that it gets really cold. Like are we talking 10°F?"

"That might be the high on a good day." Part of living in North Dakota was dealing in extreme temperatures. All year-round.

"10? As a high? On a good day?" She swallowed and gave an exaggerated shudder. "That's exactly why I was afraid to ask. I don't think I brought enough clothes. Maybe I should start making a list of my own." She pulled out her cell phone and did some scrolling and clicking before she started typing with her fingers.

"You might want to put blankets on that, and my sister always likes to have a candle burning, because it gets dark. But of course, you've already noticed that."

She didn't look up. Her thumbs kept flying over her phone. "Now that you mention it, I have felt like it's been a little bit gloomy, and I suppose it's because of the late mornings and early evenings."

"That's gonna get worse before it gets better."

"Thanks for the warning. Maybe a wax melter and some extra lights."

"Great idea. Although you might want to hold off on the lights. I suppose you can store them in your cabin. It might be a little bit until I have the electricity fixed. Same supply chain issues." He hadn't wanted to dump everything on her at once.

"Nice." Her voice was sarcastic. She kept tapping on her phone.

"Also, I'm responsible for plowing the snow, which I'll be able to do with my pickup, unless we get a couple feet or more. Then we'll have to wait for one of my brothers to come get us plowed out with something a little bigger, and we'll probably be at the bottom of their list. So—"

"Elaine told me I might as well prepare to be snowed in for several days. But I'm glad you mentioned it. I'll stock up on groceries if you think we're going to have enough room in your truck to haul everything."

"There's plenty of room. We have the whole bed."

"I thought you were getting a mattress?"

"I am. There should still be plenty of room," he insisted. The mattress could be strapped straight up, leaving most of the bed for everything else.

He pulled out his own notebook and made a note to make sure that the gas tank for his cabin had been filled up. A fireplace would be nice on a long evening, especially with three boys. They could read some around it. It might almost feel like a family. Kinda crazy how his mind had shifted so easily from single man with no dependents to family man with children and...a movie star...living in his house, which was hardly a family man thing, but that was his life.

"How do you feel about dogs?"

Her head jerked up, and she looked around, maybe responding to his lower voice or him moving closer. He tried to keep his eyes from dropping to her lips.

"Dogs? Are there wild dogs around?"

"Wolves maybe. I meant as a pet. Inside."

"Wolves?" She seemed to want to park there, but then his question seemed to penetrate her mind. "You're getting me a dog?"

"No." He allowed himself a little smile. After all, he'd just met her yesterday. He was hardly buying her gifts. He wouldn't even consider her a friend, let alone someone he knew well enough that he wanted to get a gift for her. "I don't think that anyone meant any harm by what happened at your cabin. But Rem suggested a dog might be a good idea, and since we have permission from the owner to have a dog in our cabin, and I'm definitely down for it, too, I figured I would ask around the town and see if anyone has one they wanted to give away before I looked into other angles. But I'd definitely like to get one."

"So...a dog to protect from intruders?" she asked, and the threat of fear was in her voice.

"No. Not really. Just an extra set of eyes and ears, just something to help me keep an eye out." He lifted a shoulder, keeping his voice low so the boys, who were getting more and more excited as the snow became thicker, didn't hear. "I thought it might be nice for the kids as well."

He could almost see her mind shift. "I... I don't want to pry, well, actually I do want to pry. I'm curious about the boys."

"Maybe we can talk about them. Now's not a great time."

She nodded, and then she gave an airy little shrug. "I've always wanted a dog. But I've never had one. I guess I just felt like I was working too hard to give one the attention they need. I think it would be fun."

She'd never had a dog? But she wanted one? That seemed a little foreign, especially since he'd figured she got whatever she wanted.

He was figuring out there was more to her than he'd suspected. Interesting.

Chapter 11

Going out of your way to do something special for your spouse.
- Jill Tatum

A dog was definitely a bad idea.

Bellamy stood back while Calvin, Cruz, and Cayson laughed and giggled as an over-caffeinated, way too eager and friendly, and even more hairy than necessary dog wiggled and jiggled and bumped between the three of them, slobbering everywhere and licking faces. In her excitement, she knocked a coffee cup off the coffee table and flopped into Cayson, almost knocking him down.

Bellamy had taken a step forward with her arms out to catch him, but he righted himself by grabbing a hold of the dog's fur. The dog, whose owner had said was named Crosby, did not turn around and did not growl or nip at the boys like Bellamy had been afraid she might, but instead seemed to know that the boy needed a leg up and pulled against him before turning and slobbering a big tongue all over his face.

Maybe she couldn't handle a dog after all.

Especially not one this size.

"She's about one hundred and fifty pounds. That's the St. Bernard coming out in her," the old lady said. "She's got some German Shepherd in her too."

"She probably gets that energy from the German Shepherd. A St. Bernard's pretty laid-back." Calhoun seemed decidedly unmoved by the antics of the dog. Definitely not as concerned as she thought he should be.

He should be shaking his head no, saying there was no way they were going to want a dog that size in their house. She was the size of a small elephant. They might as well have a jungle animal in their cabin.

But he said nothing of the sort, and the boys, on their knees, struggled to get their arms around her and bury their heads in her fur.

Her heart melted at the sight. Whatever the boys' story was, there was something heartrending about the sight of three little kids who just wanted love and attention.

Where was their mother? And why was Calhoun acting like he had nothing for them, since they'd already stopped at the store and bought what basically amounted to entire wardrobes for all of them, along with toothbrushes, toothpaste, coats, and enough pencils and pens and paper and crayons and scissors to start a small school.

Calhoun had asked about a dog everywhere they'd gone, and someone had suggested that Mrs. Wade, whose husband had just been sent to a nursing home, had been looking for a home for their pet.

"I know it seems like she has a lot of energy, but she settles down real nice and sleeps a lot." Mrs. Wade seemed to be worried that Calhoun might not take the dog. "I just can't take her walking like she needs. I can't keep my balance without my walker, and when it snows, I'm afraid I'll fall. I was going to take her to the pound. That's where she's going if you don't take her today."

"We have to take her. She has a C name!" Calvin cried out, and if Bellamy had wondered if the boys were listening, that answered her question right there. They might seem like they weren't paying attention, but Calvin at least always knew what was going on.

"I suppose you're right," Calhoun said indulgently.

Crosby. Who named a dog Crosby?

Calhoun looked up from the dog, his eyes finding hers where she stood over against the wall slightly out of the way. She figured this wasn't her decision to make, since she wasn't a part of this small...family, or whatever it was that Calhoun had with the boys.

"You think you're going to be able to handle all of this?" Calhoun asked, almost as though he knew what had been going on in her head.

She wanted to be honest. And a "no" sprang to her lips immediately, but it just didn't seem to be able to come out.

Could she handle it? After all, it was only for the next two months. It would be unfair of her to veto something that would give the boys such pleasure for years to come, just to make herself comfortable for the next two months.

And life wasn't supposed to be about her comfort anyway. Right?

Wasn't that part of what she wanted to get out of Hollywood for?

Wasn't the idea that everything had been about her, and what she wanted, and catering to herself, until she actually believed that she deserved everything that everybody gave her, and said about her, and started to become a person that even she didn't like.

"I think if the boys love her, we should get her. I think it will go a long way toward making them happy, and I think maybe the boys can go a long way toward making that dog happy too."

His eyes narrowed a little, like he wasn't expecting that from her at all, and why should he? It wasn't something she had expected to say. But again, she'd been trying to learn that life was more than just about her convenience. About what was easy and fun for her.

This was a start. Being humble. Putting others first. Taking on a little extra work, especially if it made someone else, or three someones, four if one included the dog, happy.

Chapter 12

Look at your spouse through God's eyes. I'll admit that one is hard!
- Maria McGee from Georgia

"**I**f the little lady says you can, you gotta listen to her. If Mama ain't happy, ain't nobody happy," Mrs. Wade said with a sly grin on her face.

Calhoun figured Mrs. Wade had no idea what was going on with Bellamy and him, but she'd probably be making a run to the Piece Makers as soon as they left so she could get the scoop.

"I guess I want to keep the little lady happy," Calhoun said, sharing a grin with Bellamy. At least she didn't get offended. She'd been smiling, or he wouldn't have said anything.

Their gazes caught and held a little, and maybe it was Mrs. Wade's words, implying that they were more than just two strangers who had bumped into each other for a little while and would bump along together until they separated and never saw each other again.

His throat started to close at the thought they would separate and never see each other again. He blinked and turned his gaze away.

"We'll take the dog. Do you have any dog food that she's used to eating?" She obviously didn't have a problem being picky about her food. He petted her, and even under all that hair, she had plenty of meat on her bones.

"I'll show you where the dog food is. I even have a leash and collar. One of those fancy retractable leashes. You can have her pans too."

That was great, because Calhoun hadn't thought to put anything that the dog might need on his list. And they'd already stopped at all the stores.

"Does she have a dog bed?"

"I want her to sleep with me!" Cayson called out. "I can sleep in my own bed if Crosby sleeps with me!"

"No! Crosby sleeps with me," Cruz said, his hands and face buried in all the dog hair, and Crosby's head curled around him like she was hugging him.

Meanwhile, Calvin stood with his hands in his pockets, his face serious. "I guess the boys can sleep with her. But I kinda would like to, too."

"Maybe, instead of getting a single mattress, I should have gotten a king-sized mattress and just had all four of you sleeping on the same bed."

"Yeah! That would be awesome!" Cayson said, jumping up and down.

Cruz looked up and smiled, and Calvin said, "I wouldn't mind that."

"You guys can't all sleep in the same bed." Bellamy sounded shocked.

She must have been terribly shocked, since, from what Calhoun had noticed, she tried to stay back and let him handle the boys. He appreciated that, that she wasn't butting into the stuff that didn't really concern her, although he didn't mind her woman's perspective. Since he was obviously lacking that.

"Actually, I'm making the bed. Why not?" He made some calculations in his head, since he'd already purchased the boards. He also had some scraps lying around, and he was pretty sure he could make a bed that would work for all three boys and the dog if he put all the mattresses together. It actually might be a good idea. Although, he might have to do some measuring so the sheets would fit.

He looked at Bellamy. "Can you use flat sheets as fitted sheets?"

Her eyes widened, and she looked a little panicked. "I don't know? Probably?"

Then he remembered she was a movie star and probably never made her own bed. But she had to come from somewhere. Surely she'd made her bed growing up. Maybe it was time he and Bellamy got to know each other a little better.

"Never mind. Let's just assume you can." He grinned. Like it was going to be a great adventure.

The panic left her eyes, and she smiled back, a little uncertain. "That look scares me a little."

"Maybe it should." He grinned even bigger, then turned to Mrs. Wade, ready to sort out whatever they needed to regarding Crosby, because he was ready to take his makeshift faux family home with him.

Chapter 13

Bellamy opened bleary eyes toward her clock and slapped a clumsy hand at the beeping item that had disturbed her slumber.

Why had she set the alarm for eight o'clock again?

Oh yeah, Calhoun had asked her if she would keep an eye on the boys if he got them started on their school so he could go to her cabin and see if there was some way he could possibly piece her plumbing together.

She wanted to talk to him and thought he had wanted the same after his comment yesterday, but by the time they got home and got everything unloaded and Calhoun had cooked supper, it had been late. Everyone had been tired, including her, who was usually a night owl.

At least she wasn't having any trouble sleeping, even if she wasn't getting the rest and relaxation during the day that she'd intended.

At least all the activity had kept her mind off the divorce, the movie, and Houston.

His name didn't elicit any kind of longing, only a general sense of disgust.

Climbing groggily out of bed, Bellamy stumbled to the restroom, threw her hair up in a ponytail without brushing it, and did a very, very scaled-down version of her morning routine.

She had turned off all her notifications, and this was the second morning in a row she hadn't started her day by checking in online.

Yesterday, she hadn't missed it at all.

Today, she was actually eager not to have it. Funny how her soul just felt lighter without the heaviness that was social media.

A part of her did wonder what effect her disappearance would have on the world, or at least on her corner of it, but she didn't wonder hard enough to actually want to pick up her phone and find out. In fact, she left her phone in her room as she walked down the stairs.

Calhoun had all three boys sitting at the table already, all three of them with books open in front of them. And the house smelled deliciously of bacon.

She hadn't had bacon in ages.

Crosby, who had apparently been making rounds around the table, lunged over across the living room to the stairs, shoving into Bellamy and insisting that she be petted.

Bellamy laughed and crouched, scratching the furry head and allowing the slobbering tongue to lick over her cheek.

It looked like everyone had eaten and was already started on their schoolwork. She straightened. The dog pushed against her legs as she walked across the living room to the table.

"Wow. Am I late?"

He had said sometime after eight.

He shook his head. "No. But I hope you don't mind we didn't hold breakfast for you. I hated to start the boys on their schoolwork without feeding them first. Did we wake you?"

"No. I didn't hear a thing until my alarm."

He grinned, and the boys grinned with him.

The littlest boy seemed to have trouble sitting still and wiggled a good bit, but his brows were scrunched in concentration, and he gripped his pencil tightly.

They hadn't been able to find a lot of books that worked for them, but there had been enough homeschoolers in the area that they found some things that worked at the new used bookstore that had apparently opened not long ago in Sweet Water.

"Palmer or Ames might be around today to drop off the school-books they said we could use," Calhoun reminded her as she walked over to the kitchen.

"I remember." She scrunched up her nose. "But they said something about a storm?"

"It's North Dakota. We always have storms." His words were dismissive, even though he'd already warned her that if they got more than a foot or so of snow, they'd be snowed in for a while.

He straightened from where he'd been bending over Cruz's shoulder pointing at something on the paper and speaking softly in his ear.

"I have some bacon underneath that lid right there, and if you want me to throw a couple of eggs on the skillet, I can. Those are no good cold, so I didn't cook you any when I was cooking earlier."

Eggs sounded divine, but she said, "I'll make do with the bacon. I don't want to put you out."

"It's not a problem."

She shook her head. "You wanted to get some stuff done over at my cabin. I don't want to hold you up."

He looked at her for a minute, and she wondered if maybe she should be more clear. She didn't want him to get the idea that it was a problem for her to be staying here. It wasn't for her. In fact, having the boys and Crosby to distract her had been a real blessing.

Of course, most of her thoughts had centered on Calhoun. She'd never met a man quite like him. Someone who seemed so capable, who could do plumbing and electrical work and carpentry. Although she hadn't actually seen him in action, she'd seen the effects, and if these cabins were any indication, he was quite talented.

He could cook, and seemed to know what the children needed for their schooling, and had known his way around the grocery store and the used bookstore.

Watching him yesterday had opened her eyes a lot of ways. Knowing that not only had she never met a man quite like him, but that the bubble she had lived in that had felt so big was actually quite limiting. She didn't have nearly the world knowledge she'd thought.

There was a part of her that was definitely interested in learning more about him.

And there was another part that wanted to have nothing to do with another man. No matter how different he was from the men she had known.

"All right. But they're there if you want to make yourself some," he finally said, and she had to clamp her lips around the words that wanted to tumble out. Words to explain that she wasn't in a big rush to move out, that she just didn't want to be a burden to him. Or maybe, that she didn't want to fall in love with anyone or anything else. Not just with Calhoun. The boys were a temptation, sweet as they were.

Calhoun himself was an even bigger temptation.

"How long do you think you'll be?" she asked, wanting to move on for some reason. She didn't want to examine her feelings, and she definitely didn't want to have to explain them. The entire world had already picked them apart and decided that they knew her motivations, and her expectations, and why she did everything that she did. Most of the time, they assigned something negative to her and assumed the worst about her.

She wanted to protect herself.

"Not long. I'm not expecting to find anything new today that I didn't see yesterday, but I got a couple of things that I thought might possibly work in the meantime. I wanted to try them. If they don't work, I won't be long at all. Maybe an hour. Even if they do, I'll make sure I come back for lunch." He scratched his head, looked down at the floor. Finally, he looked back up. "I... I got the feeling you don't cook much."

"That's right. I'm sorry. I can make a good salad, and I know some really great restaurants in LA."

"Yeah."

He didn't say anything else. Nothing like *that won't be a big help for us right now.* Or *do you know any other worthless skills?*

She supposed she appreciated his lack of sarcasm.

That was something else that she'd noticed as she walked beside him yesterday. He had a humility that was attractive. He didn't seem to need to work to make himself look good, or even care how he looked. Not physically, but how he came off to the world. His lack of guile, lack of putting on any kind of show, had intrigued her. She wasn't sure she'd ever met a man who was more real.

"Hey," he said softly.

Her head jerked. She hadn't realized she'd crossed her arms over her chest and had just been staring at the floor. Feeling like she once again wasn't good enough.

"What?" She blinked. She'd forgotten where she was.

"It's fine. You have other things you do well. Things I can't even imagine. It's okay."

She focused on keeping her mouth from dropping open. Had he read all of that on her face? Regardless, he didn't seem like the kind of man who was sensitive and caring, although the way he'd been with the boys, firm and kind, had been exactly what they needed.

"I guess."

Regardless of how caring he was, the fact remained that the skills she had were not helpful for living life. They were good for playing pretend on movie screens, but when it came to being able to, oh, say, keep a marriage together, she stunk.

And she had a track record to prove it.

"I don't have to go," he said, walking closer but still giving her space. On the one hand, she appreciated that space; on the other, she really wanted to lay her head on his chest and rest in his arms, and she had no clue where that idea came from.

"No. Go on. I've got this. I am capable of reading and writing and doing simple math. I'm pretty sure I can handle this."

How hard could it be?

He jerked his head and dropped his arms, shoving them in his pockets and turning. He walked over to the boys and gave them a few last instructions, pointing to something on Cruz's paper and telling him he did a good job.

Then he walked to the door, put his coat and hat on, and, with his hand on the doorknob, turned around.

"Do you want me to take Crosby with me? So far, she's been house-trained, but I've kept a close eye on her."

All three boys looked up when he asked, and they turned pleading eyes to her. None of them said anything, but they didn't need to. She could read their expressions clearly. They wanted the dog to stay.

"I think I can handle it."

He walked out, and she felt strangely bereft. She ignored that, put the rest of the bacon she held in her mouth, and walked over to the table, walking behind the boys' chairs, as she had seen Calhoun do.

Noticing the little boy was wiggling even more, she said, "Are you okay, Cayson?"

"This is hard. I don't want to do it anymore!" he burst out, making Bellamy want to laugh on one hand and cry on the other. She also wanted to ask *why couldn't you have said that three minutes ago when Calhoun was still in here and would have known what to say?*

"Maybe I can help you with something?" She walked over and stood behind him.

"No! It's too hard!" Cayson threw his pencil down. It bounced on the table, rolled, and fell off the other side. Crosby happened to be standing right beside it, and she picked it up and held it in her mouth.

"Crosby! No!" Bellamy said before she heard a crunching sound that was most definitely the pencil being chewed in their dog's mouth.

"Crosby! Put it down!" Bellamy said, hurrying around the table to get the pencil, or what was left of it, from the dog's mouth. She wasn't sure what pencil splinters did to a dog's insides, but she kinda figured a vet would probably have to be involved.

She dropped to her knees, shoving her hand into the dog's mouth and hoping it didn't all of a sudden decide to bite her. She pulled the pieces out as well as she could, setting the slobber-covered splinters in her lap so she could take them to the garbage can.

She pulled out the last piece, patting Crosby on the head and standing back up, making a mental note to make sure no pencils were left lying around on the floor. Looking over the table, she was dismayed to see that Cruz had completely stopped doing his work and was now wrestling Cayson, their arms locked together, as each one was apparently attempting to be the first one to knock his brother off his chair.

Calvin wasn't wrestling, but his pencil was lying on his book, and he was no longer working but watching his brothers with a grin.

"Boys," she said, not loud, but as firmly as she could, which didn't sound very firm to her. She'd never dealt with children before. Funny that she'd been married five times, but never long enough for her and whichever husband she was with to think about kids.

Thankfully, she supposed. Although, the idea of having a normal family was something that elicited a longing in her chest.

But, while Calhoun had seemed to have complete control, in the short ten minutes he'd been gone, she'd lost it, because the boys ignored her word and continued wrestling.

"Cruz. Cayson. You boys are not doing your schoolwork."

"Cayson said it was too hard. And mine is too," Calvin said while the other two boys kept tussling.

"Why didn't you tell Mr. Calhoun that when he was here?"

"Because it wasn't too hard then," Calvin said like the answer should have been obvious, his eyes never leaving his brothers.

Cruz seemed to be on the verge of knocking Cayson off his chair. Calvin shoved his own chair back and hurried to help his brother. Grabbing a hold of Cruz, he and Cayson threw him down to the floor. They cheered, which caused Crosby to start barking and dancing all around them.

Cruz yelled, and Bellamy was sure he'd broken something with the way he landed, but thankfully he popped back up, grabbing a hold of Calvin in a headlock, trying to jerk him down, apparently getting the upper hand by catching Calvin off guard.

Cayson took the opportunity to yell and try to grab hold of the dog and run around the table, avoiding Bellamy who reached out to try to grab either the boy or the dog, she wasn't sure. At this point, either one would have been fine.

She missed both, coming up with just a handful of hair, while Calvin body-slammed Cruz to the floor. Cruz didn't pop up quite as quickly that time, and Calvin yelled, beating his fist on his chest, then laughing as Cayson and the dog ran by him.

He turned around and started chasing them. Rather than going around in a circle, they cut through the living room, stepped over the coffee table, ran over the couch, and used the end table as a jumping-off point, with Calvin following along behind, only when he got to the end table and jumped, he ducked his body and did a flip, landing on the back of his neck on the couch. He shouted then grunted before rolling over.

Bellamy almost swallowed her tongue. She thought for sure the kid was going to break his neck.

But she realized that somehow the entire box of new pencils had spilled to the floor, and when she'd grabbed at Crosby, she'd dropped all the pieces she'd just picked up, so now there were slobbery pencil pieces on the floor, along with brand-new pencils rolling everywhere. There was also paper scattered over the table, she wasn't sure quite when that happened, and boys running everywhere, along with the dog, and it felt more like four boys. Or twenty.

She was supposed to be in charge of this chaos.

She wanted to cry. She had no idea how to stop everything.

If you can't beat them, join them.

She wasn't sure where that advice came from, but she'd heard it somewhere before, and it seemed very applicable now.

So she ran over to the steps, yelling, "Watch this, boys!" as she jumped up five steps, then turned around and jumped down, realizing as she did so that the last time she'd done anything like this, she'd been a teenager, and it had been a lot easier.

She barely missed the last step and fell forward.

But the boys didn't notice. They cheered and piled on the stairs, each of them trying to jump from higher and higher up.

Every time they jumped, somehow they managed to land on their feet and do a running turn around the dining room table. Every once in a while, they took a detour into the kitchen and grabbed a piece of bacon off the dwindling pile on the plate on the counter, and then they'd run across the couch in the living room, past the coffee table, jump on the end table, and Calvin and Cruz would do flips as they landed on the couch before they went back to the stairs.

So far, Cayson hadn't managed to do a flip, and he wasn't quite able to go up as high as the other boys could on the stairs.

Definitely joining them was easier than trying to contain them, and Bellamy realized after a while she was actually having fun. She was also able to lead them, in a roundabout way, which gave her an illusion of control.

But they were soon bored with jumping on the stairs, so she grabbed the four corners of her bedsheet and held it in one hand while stepping over the railing at the top of the stairs with the other.

Calvin had suggested jumping off of the railing at the top, and she wanted to say it was too dangerous, but then she decided she could just go first and try it out for them.

Cruz was the one who suggested a parachute. That's why her bed things were scattered everywhere, over the railing and partway down the stairs, as she held the sheet in one hand, the railing in the other, and looked down at the floor which seemed strangely farther away than it should.

There were two seconds of silence while the boys waited for her to jump with baited breath, and that's when the door opened and Calhoun stepped back in.

Bellamy, hanging onto the railing with one hand, holding the four corners of her bedsheet with the other, one toe dangling over the open air, froze with wide eyes.

Cruz was right behind her, on the other side of the railing. Calvin had just finished a jump and a flip and was lying on his back on the couch looking up, waiting for her to jump.

Cayson was munching on a piece of bacon and was standing on the table. He was the only thing on the table, and Bellamy honestly wasn't quite sure where the schoolbooks had gone.

Crosby, as though aware that possibly their antics weren't going to be met with approval, and possibly having experience in that very thing, slunk down the stairs, her tail between her legs, her butt wiggling back and forth as she went to greet Calhoun.

Calhoun blinked twice, opened his mouth, paused, then slowly closed the door behind him, ignoring the dog, his eyes sweeping the room, then landing back on Bellamy.

"If you're giving a lesson on gravity, I suggest using an apple."

Chapter 14

Believing your vows! And not thinking of divorce as an option!
- Shelia Garrison from North Carolina

"So can you tell me again why you were hanging from the banister when I walked in today?" Calhoun asked, his hands shoved in the pockets of his coat as his butt leaned against the railing of the cabin, the wide North Dakota night sky spread out above them, beautiful, clear, and shimmering with stars and deep velvet darkness.

Bellamy huddled in her jacket on the other end of the small porch, leaning against the railing facing him.

They hadn't spoken about anything that had happened for the rest of the day. They just cleaned up the mess together and got the boys settled down again, with Bellamy sitting with Cruz on the couch listening to his reading lesson.

The rest of the day had gone fairly smoothly, with him having the boys helping him during the afternoon. Bellamy had managed to heat up some canned soup on the stove without burning it.

The same couldn't be said for the bread she had attempted, but they'd taken the burnt outside off, and the inside was still good.

The boys were now in bed, and he'd asked Bellamy if he could talk to her.

"I'm sorry. I just...lost control like two seconds after you left, and rather than fighting them, I figured I'd join them. I got a little carried away. I...have a tendency to get carried away."

"Is that what you call it? Thinking you can fly? That's a tendency to get 'carried away' that I'd maybe get some professional help for."

She snorted, and he was glad his words had come out the way he'd meant them. Not accusing her of anything, but acknowledging that there was room for improvement.

A lot of room.

He apparently could improve in a lot of areas as well. Like his ability to talk to this woman. He just couldn't seem to figure out what he wanted to say.

He had questions tumbling over themselves in his head. And he had his brain telling him he needed to get away from her. She was dangerous to him.

But he had another part of him wanting to get closer. Wanting to touch her. Wanting to...

He shook the thoughts away.

"It's understandable that you've never been around children before. I guess I really never have either, but I had a lot of siblings."

"I was an only child."

Her voice was soft and a little sad. Made him think that maybe she had longed for siblings. Or maybe there was something else.

Why not ask?

"Why does that thought make you sad?" He wasn't used to talking about feelings and definitely wasn't used to wondering about them. But Bellamy was different. Different in a way he couldn't explain.

She shrugged. The night was still and quiet, with just a breeze blowing, but it barely made a sound.

Finally she said, "My mom aborted my two older siblings. I didn't know that until I was eighteen. I think my childhood would have been a lot less lonely, but maybe I wouldn't have been around."

He understood what she was saying. One small decision could ripple through a person's life, changing everything. A decision to stay home or to go out. A decision to take a job or not. A decision to...get closer to someone.

"You'd be a different person."

"I know."

"I know you're wondering about the boys. I'm sorry I haven't seemed to have a chance to explain to you about them until now."

"You're going to explain?" she asked, interest lacing every syllable.

"A woman I had gone to school with dropped them off at the garage, claiming that Calvin was mine."

"And you're saying he's not?" she asked, a bit of derision in her voice, like his denial was typical. A man not wanting to take responsibility.

So he did something he normally would never do.

"When I was fifteen, I made a vow. A vow to the Lord. I promised that I would wait for the girl He had for me. I told Him however long it took, I'd wait. But I asked Him to send me His very best. In the meantime, I promised to become the best man I could while I was waiting."

There was silence for a bit, and he figured he'd probably shocked her. That wasn't the type of thing that people, men, normally did these days, and most definitely not men from her circles.

She would never understand. Not why he did it, nor why he kept it. That a vow meant something to him. It was sacred. Especially a vow made to the Lord. He wasn't going to break it.

He'd been tempted. Lonely. Begging God to move. To give him what he longed for.

But, in the end, a man was only as good as his word.

Calhoun kept his.

He didn't expect Bellamy to understand.

"Wow," she breathed. "That's... I've never heard of anything like that. Not in modern days anyway. Maybe in stories."

"Yeah." What else was there to say? Sometimes he felt stupid. He was pretty sure she, along with most of society, considered him stupid.

"You and I are the opposite. I just signed the papers for my fifth divorce. I'm probably younger than you are."

"Never too late to make a vow. Start where you're at. I just happened to start at the beginning. If you mess up, start again. You just start where you are. Draw a line, make that your new beginning.

God takes... God *wants* whatever you're willing to give. Actually, He wants everything."

"That's too much."

"He gave everything for you."

"It's been a long time since I've heard that."

"So you have heard it?"

"On my grandparents' farm, back when I visited them as a kid. They lived in Nebraska. It's a completely different world from LA. But they both died when I was little."

"Too bad. Grandparents are fun."

"Yeah. But I think Mom pretty much did the opposite of everything they taught her. Then I picked up where she left off, I guess."

"Don't be too hard on yourself. Like I said, right now, this second is the start of the rest of your life."

She hugged her arms around herself and turned so that her hip was leaning against the banister, and she looked out away from the house. Out into the vast darkness before lifting her head and looking up at the stars.

"It sounds good when you put it that way." But then she seemed to shake herself, and she said, "So Calvin's not yours?" And this time when she said it, it sounded like she believed him.

"He wasn't. But..."

Again, he didn't typically go around talking about his mom. He didn't talk about his vow either. No one knew. That was between God and him. And now Bellamy.

Now, he was seriously contemplating talking about his mother. Another secret subject.

"My mom ran off with another man when my brothers and I were small. My sister was young, really young. That marks a kid. To know your mom doesn't want you. That she'd walk away, not ever care. It's tough. And that woman, Maci, came in, accusing me of fathering Calvin, but basically what she wanted was to dump her boys on me. They knew it."

"They were there?"

"Yeah. I knew how they felt. Their mom didn't want them. My brothers and I, my little sister, felt the same way. Dad is not the most nurturing person in the world, but at least we knew he wanted us. Those boys, they didn't have anyone."

"Was she running off with another man too?"

"Yeah. I guess. Said something about going on a motorcycle tour around the country with her boyfriend."

"Wow. I guess I always thought someday I'd be a mom. I just can't imagine leaving my kids."

"Yeah. But kids are hard. You saw that today. I suppose it's natural for people to get tired and to want a break."

"I think you're a little too forgiving. She was walking away from her kids! She doesn't deserve grace."

"I don't deserve grace, but God gave it to me anyway. I suppose the very least I can do is try to extend it to people that are around me. Even, or maybe especially, to the people I feel don't deserve it. Because, whatever they've done, in God's eyes, I've been just as bad."

"You talk about that like you believe it."

"I do."

She didn't argue. Probably there was no point. Maybe she hadn't been around long enough to know that's how he lived his life, but maybe she was figuring it out.

"So you just let her tell you that you were the father, and you didn't argue?"

He'd wanted to argue. Had to fight himself not to, but in the end... "Sometimes *doing* right is more important than *being* right. I felt it was right, felt the Lord was putting those boys in my path for a reason. Maybe there was something I had been through in my life, with my mom leaving me, that would allow me to help them."

"But you have all this work to do in the cabins." She'd seen the other cabins, probably hadn't seen the insides and the work that needed to be done there, but he was gratified that she at least knew he hadn't been sitting around wanting something to do, but had been busy, and taking the boys had been a sacrifice.

"When God puts something in your path for you to do, you need to do it. Because the work God gives you is eternal work. With repercussions that last for eternity. That's far more important, although it seems less urgent than the normal everyday work we have." He didn't know how else to explain it. "Sometimes we get so focused on what we want or what we think is going to make us look good—to other people—and we ignore the things, or don't even see them, that God has given us to do. The people He's given us to love and care for. To be true friends to. To sacrifice for." He lapsed into silence, unsure how to convince anyone that sometimes the things that looked obvious were often just red herrings.

"I see. That seems so wise, and so obvious now, but I've never thought of that."

They were quiet for a few minutes, Calhoun thinking that he didn't feel wise.

He felt lonely.

Odd, since often when he stood beneath the wide North Dakota sky, he felt closer to God than any other time. But tonight, it seemed to stir some kind of longing in him, some kind of soul-empty feeling that he couldn't articulate, couldn't quite grasp.

"So you took the boys?"

"Yeah." He put a hand up and hooked it around his neck, leaning back and looking up. "I pretty much demanded all three of them. I insisted on guardianship, which I got, and I wanted permanent custody. Unsurprisingly, I haven't heard anything from Maci since I was granted guardianship and she split. I hate that the boys' future is in limbo like that. At least when my mom left, I still had something that felt a little solid with my dad in the picture along with my brothers around me and my sister.

"We had a business. The business Dad had since we were born. Things that were permanent. These boys' lives...they don't have anything. Other than each other."

"Yeah. I see. I guess... I guess I'm kind of surprised that you saw all of that."

"I suppose I didn't want to waste the trial that God had put me through. My mom left. I can understand how that feels and put myself in someone else's shoes. Hopefully anyway."

"Don't waste trials. That's new too."

He grunted out a laugh. "Most people don't see trials as things that are beneficial. But, even if you mess your trial up and don't go through it very well, there are still lessons to be learned. And the more lessons you learn, maybe the better you go through each trial you have."

"I don't want trials. I want peace. Just peace for the rest of my life."

"Even if you moved to a deserted island, lived by yourself, had food air-dropped to you, you wouldn't have peace. There'd always be something. You might as well face that and then decide that you want to develop the kind of character that allows you to face your trials with courage and conviction, morals and values, so that you can rest in the peaceful times, because there will be peaceful times, with the satisfaction that you've done the best you can."

"Really? You really think it's impossible to have a life of peace?"

That was one thing in life that he was absolutely certain about. "There will always be conflict. Trauma. Hard times. Always."

"That's negative."

"You disagree? Convince me you're right."

Her mouth opened as she stared at him. Turning full toward him, she crossed her arms. He guessed she wasn't used to being invited to convince someone that they were wrong.

After a long silence that he wasn't tempted to break at all, because he figured she was going through her head, trying to figure out where he was wrong, she finally said, "I guess you're right. Times of hardship, followed by times of peace. That's life."

"Yeah. So now you know all of my times of hardship, and you know about the boys. Although, I guess I didn't tell you that the younger two aren't able to read, and Maci had been homeschooling them but not doing a very good job, which is something that gives homeschoolers a bad name—when deadbeat parents homeschool, without actually doing the work. Anyway, is it terrible of me to admit that I'm curious about you?"

Chapter 15

Concentrate on the things you like and ignore the things you don't.
- Susanne Nielsen from Idaho Falls, Idaho

"My life is an open book—it's on social media for all to see."

Bellamy wrapped her arms around her waist tightly. Grateful she brought the heavy coat. Not that she needed to be standing outside staring at the stars. Although, there was something...fun about it.

Maybe fun wasn't the word.

Cozy. Heartwarming. Intimate.

Maybe it was the company.

Most likely. But she didn't want to think that way. She'd come out here thinking she was getting away from men. Giving herself a chance to heal and figure out how to live her life without feeling like she needed a man. Wanting to put God in His rightful place in her life. The place she'd been filling up with "love" and romance. Lust.

After five husbands, she knew getting married wasn't a solution to any problems she thought she might have.

But the man beside her had integrity and character, and she owed him something.

"I need to apologize for what I did today."

"Huh?" He grunted, sounding a little surprised, almost like he'd forgotten she was there, but she also got the impression that he was shocked that she might need to apologize to him. She had felt it was obvious.

"You left me with the boys." She huffed out a breath. "I'm an adult. You had every reason to expect that there would not be chaos reigning in your house when you got back."

"Well, I have to admit I was a little surprised to see you hanging off the banister getting ready to jump from the second floor. What in the world possessed you?" He added that last question almost as an afterthought, like he might be afraid to hear the answer.

She had wanted to apologize. She had wanted to explain. But from the little she knew about him, he deserved more. At least he deserved to have her act like an adult.

Although, she couldn't remember the last time she let loose and had not cared what people thought. Or who might be catching a social media post that would go viral.

"I think... I think I panicked when I lost control of the boys. I... I seemed to have at least gotten them to listen to me a little when I suggested we do daring things. But I had to keep suggesting more and more outrageous things because I felt like if I didn't, they'd lose interest and I'd lose the little bit of control I had."

"You thought you had control?"

She crossed her arms, feeling defensive at his aghast tone. "They were following me. That was a type of control. I know it doesn't make sense. That's why I'm apologizing. I... I don't know how else to explain it, and maybe there isn't a good explanation. I just know I wasn't thinking the way I normally do. In particular, jumping off the banister is not something I've ever thought about before in my life. I can't believe I thought about it today. I just... I just didn't know what else to do."

"I see." He was quiet for a bit, almost as though he were considering what she said. She'd never had someone who seemed to listen to her the way he did. "I think it was my fault for asking you to watch them in the first place."

"No!"

He held up a hand, dim in the darkness. "Just listen. I pulled you out of your comfort zone. I mean, you're already out of your comfort zone here in North Dakota. And here in the cabins away from everyone. That's another step outside of it. Then, I leave you with three boys, when you've never been around children before. And to make things worse, the boys were out of their comfort zones as well."

He shifted, almost as though he were agitated. "But I was talking like I felt like you owed me an apology to begin with, and you didn't. You didn't do anything wrong. No one got hurt, and maybe you were being a little bit crazier than most adults would think is acceptable, but your explanation made sense to me, and I feel like maybe you just lost your head for a bit, because of the reasons I said."

He was giving her grace that she didn't deserve. He should be telling her how he would never trust her with the boys again. How she wasn't responsible enough to babysit a pet turtle, let alone little humans. Instead, he thought of all the reasons why she might not have been at her best and accepted her explanation as truth and fact.

"I'm not sure I've ever had anyone look at me and see good the way you seem to."

Maybe she shouldn't have said that, because it caused him to shift again, like she'd made him uncomfortable. But it was true.

"Guess I've just been thinking about what you've been through, all that I know about it is from what I've heard and the little that I've read. And it seems to me that maybe you had a pretty tough time. Someone needs to be on your side."

She thought of all her friends in LA. And she did have some good friends. People who had stood by her. Still, this man seemed different. Because he didn't seem like he was trying to convince her that he liked her, and he wasn't just blindly being loyal because that was what was expected of him.

"You're different than most of the people I know." All of the people she knew.

He grunted. "Yeah. That's a polite way of saying I'm weird. It's okay. But I thought we were talking about you now. After all, we've already talked about me."

She laughed, feeling somehow lighter than she had in a very long time. "There's nothing I can say about me that you can't read online somewhere. And maybe that was another thing about today. I'd left my phone in my room when I walked out of it this morning, and I never gave it another thought all day long. Do you know how long it's been since I haven't checked social media for an entire day?"

"That's sad." He sounded like it really was.

"Yeah. Are you on social media?" She wasn't sure where that question came from. Everybody was. But just from the way he said it, it sounded like—

"Nah. Never took the time to figure it out. The people I want to talk to are right here in my life. I can text them. I do know how to do that."

"Wow."

"I know. Why do you keep changing the subject and making this conversation about me?"

"Because there's nothing I can tell you that you can't find out online. I told you that."

"I told you I'm not online. Not much anyway." He turned, taking a step so he stood at the top of the steps leading to the porch, and leaned his shoulder against the porch post, looking up at the sparkling stars. "There's the Big Dipper."

She moved so she was standing against the other porch post, several feet still separating them, but they weren't standing on the opposite ends of the porch like they were getting ready to have a shootout once the moon came up or something.

"I see it. I can't believe how clear the stars are out here."

"Yeah. I think being out here helps everything become a little bit more clear. Things we think are really important when we're boxed up next to people, with no elbow room, aren't quite so important when we see how small we are and how big God is."

She hadn't thought about it that way, but maybe that was why she was almost driven to come here, to get away from the city, to be able to hear herself think again, and to find the pieces that she'd lost.

"The last movie I made, I made with my ex-husband. I agreed to make the movie with him while we were still married, and I couldn't back out when I found him having an affair with my assistant."

"What is it that men can't seem to resist about assistants?"

She laughed. She figured he'd intended for her to. It was true. How many famous people had she heard about whose husband or significant other had been carrying on with the assistant behind their back? It happened all the time.

"I guess there was a lot of pressure on me, and my assistant was just doing a job. And my ex is very charming." She snorted. "My assistant was a flirt, too. I guess I knew that."

"I always wondered why famous people hire good-looking nannies and assistants. Seems like you'd want to hire someone old and trustworthy, someone who is obviously in the job because they love the job, or love you, rather than someone who is struggling to make it in the same business you are, stealing your contacts—"

"And my husband."

"Exactly."

"Maybe it doesn't have anything to do with the assistant. Maybe men just are incapable of being loyal?"

She hated the bitterness in her voice. But wasn't that the truth? It shouldn't matter what kind of assistant she had. She should be able to have the most beautiful assistant in the world. Her assistant should be able to flirt, wear suggestive clothing, and give all the sweet compliments in the world, attempting to stroke the man's ego, and *it shouldn't matter*.

"Ouch," Calhoun said, humor in his voice, but she figured she probably had offended him, too.

"Sorry. I guess I just tried five times. Stupidly. I should have learned after the first one or at least the second. But no, I keep thinking that I'd find someone who could actually be true. Who wouldn't be swayed by pretty words that stroked his ego, flirting glances, or a sweet little sob story and batting eyelashes. But I guess it doesn't matter. After all, it looks like I have everything, doesn't it? And no matter what I do, my assistant will always be the underdog. Just because I'm successful, and she's not."

"I guess I can't really argue with you on some of those points. I think men really are susceptible to compliments, particularly compliments from new people. After all, men like to conquer territory, and if he already has you, your compliments are old, while your assistant hasn't been conquered yet, and...yeah. I can see that."

"Thanks. I knew I was right." She didn't want to gloat, but that's just the way men were. They got bored with one woman, and they wanted to move on to the next. They wanted the challenge, the newness, that whatever high it was that a man got from flirting and hearing someone new stroke his ego and laugh at his jokes and let him think he was protecting her, that she needed his support and help.

"Whoa. I didn't say you were right. I did say that men were susceptible. But a man of character puts up guards in his life to keep him from ever doing the things your husband did to you. Falling for the trap of pretty eyes and flirty words."

"Guards? You mean he has a bunch of rules for himself."

"You say that like it's a bad thing. How else do you stay away from things that you shouldn't be involved in? Don't you wear a seat belt to protect yourself from injury in a car accident?"

"That's different."

"Not at all. We use fences to protect our animals. We put fences around swimming pools to protect children from falling into them. We have all kinds of physical guards in our lives. Why wouldn't we have rules to keep ourselves morally straight as well?"

Bellamy stared without seeing at the far horizon. She'd never considered that. It made sense though. A person had physical boundaries to keep themself safe. Guardrails along roads. Electrical lines were either buried or put way up where people couldn't touch them.

"What type of guards are you talking about?"

He grunted, almost as though he found her question funny, when she hadn't meant it in a humorous way at all. But then he spoke, and she realized he was laughing at himself.

"Guards like never being alone with a woman they aren't married to." He grunted again. "That's one of the guards that I've had up for myself and look at me breaking it with you right now."

"I'm not married, so it's okay. I'm not saying anything would ever happen between us." She didn't want to imply that at all, because they were just discussing things, and their words were not flirty, not even a little. There was nothing suggestive about what they were talking about. "But if it did, it's okay, I'm single. You're single. We're not hurting anyone."

"Other than ourselves."

"Why? How could that hurt ourselves?"

"Well, this isn't really something you're going to hear in polite society anywhere, but when we let our guard down, when we're alone with people, we might be tempted to do things with them, things we probably shouldn't, and maybe our feelings get involved, maybe those people aren't right for us. Maybe God has someone else for us. But we've gotten sucked into the idea that the one that we've been spending a lot of time with is the one we want, so we decide we've fallen in love, and we end up with someone that if we had been thinking logically about it, we wouldn't have had anything to do with." He sighed. "That's not a very good explanation, but it's the best I can come up with. I don't want to be blinded by emotions and end up with someone that God didn't plan for me to have. I don't think I'll be happy with someone like that."

"So you're going to tell me that you've never been alone with a girl?"

"I try to avoid situations like that, yeah. Avoid them until I know for sure that the girl I'm with is the girl God wants me with."

"And how are you going to know that?" she asked. Half annoyed at him, but mostly because she wished she'd had the insight to think of that before she got married five times.

Why hadn't she considered that her emotions might be wrong? Why hadn't she looked on romance logically? But who even did that? Even talked about it?

People fall in love, they get married. That's the way it went. Except... When she thought about it, that really wasn't the way civilization had worked for most of the time that man had walked the earth. Not really. People depended on their parents to help them find a mate that was suitable. Love often didn't have anything to do with it.

"I guess I'll pray about it and hope that God lets me know."

"What's He going to do? Talk to you? Say *this is the one*?" She kind of imitated God's voice, not mocking but just allowing her disbelief to shine through.

"I guess not. He's never done that before. But you know how you just have a feeling? And you read your Bible, and it points to something, and you end up having a conversation with a friend, and that points to the same thing, and then you pray about it, and you feel peace about it, and you move forward. Because if you didn't have that peace, and you didn't have the confirmation from other Christian friends, and you didn't read that verse of the Bible that seems to be saying the same thing, that's when you know you shouldn't go forward."

"I've heard that Christians have higher divorce rates than people who aren't Christians. I guess that doesn't work for everyone."

"I don't know that all Christians wait for God to pick out their mate for them. I think a lot of them do it the way we were just talking about, become emotionally invested, because the assistant sends you a cute smile and a happy compliment and gives you a little sob story that makes you start feeling for her. And you haven't put any guards up, so you start falling for that. Christians are susceptible to that just as anyone else."

"But surely some Christians think that God has chosen their mate, and then they end up divorced. What about that?"

"We live in a fallen world. People don't always do what they're supposed to do. Maybe they got divorced when they should have stayed together. Maybe their mate left the marriage, through no fault of their own, even if he was the one that God had for them. I don't know. I wish I had all the answers. It would make my life a lot easier."

"Because you're still waiting for God to bring you someone?"

"For one."

"He's sure taking His good old time, isn't He? Maybe He's forgotten about you?"

Chapter 16

Compromise and never go to bed mad at each other.
- Jan Rexroth from York, PA

Bellamy didn't mean to mock Calhoun, she just couldn't stifle the annoyance that she hadn't been smarter when making decisions about who she would get married to. Look how she ended up.

Before he could say anything, she said, "I'm sorry. I'm irritated with myself, and I'm taking it out on you. You're making sense. I should have had more of a plan, rather than just looking around at some guy who was good looking, who I was attracted to, and who I 'fell in love with' and rushed off to marry."

"At least you got married. A lot of people don't anymore."

Her mouth dropped. Although she wasn't sure why she was surprised. With all the things that he had been saying, she should have known he would feel that way. But she had to say, "No one else understood. After all, people don't get married anymore. They just live together, trying things out for a while to see how it fits them, and then they move out or move in with someone else. I'm an anomaly, since I haven't done that but got married instead. It definitely gives people something to make fun of me for. After all, I pledged my life to five different men, and I've broken my vows every single time." She looked down at her feet, not really seeing them, just disgusted with herself.

She never thought she'd be the kind of person to break vows. She never thought she'd have five divorces under her belt before she was thirty-five.

It was hard to respect herself.

"Remember what we were saying about starting today and being the person you want to be?"

"It's like you read my mind." She lifted her head. "I hate that my life isn't what I wanted it to be."

"Mine isn't either," he offered.

"How's that? You're not looking at five failed marriages, wondering how that happened."

"I spent my twenties alone. I wasn't planning on that." He jerked his head toward the house. "Those three boys could be mine. I could have a family right now. I never thought I would stand out under the big North Dakota sky, still single, still looking, still praying that God has someone for me at my age."

He turned and looked straight at her, and the moon was bright enough that she could see a feeling that almost seemed like anguish in his eyes. "Maybe God *has* forgotten me. Maybe the woman that He had for me got tired of waiting and is with someone else now. Maybe I'll never find her. Maybe I screwed up somehow and didn't do something the Lord wanted me to do, and missed meeting her. I don't know." His lips flattened. He shook his head and looked away.

"I suppose there are a million different kinds of regret. A million different ways we think we're not good enough, or a million different ways our lives don't happen the way we want them to. And we beat ourselves up about it."

"Yeah. We forget our worth isn't in what our lives are or aren't. Whether or not they turned out the way we think they should have. They're not in what people think about us. What they look at us and see. Our worth is in our status as a child of God. In His love. That's all the worth we need. But we're always looking for something else."

"I thought I was the only one. Never satisfied. Never thinking I'm good enough."

"Far from it. But we are, because God says we are, because of Christ's sacrifice. He's made us good enough. And the love of the Creator of the universe is beaming down on us." He shook his head. "I wonder how we can even now wonder about our worth, yet we manage to."

"He lets our mistakes go faster than we do."

"That's absolutely true. Although, I think He always has lessons He wants us to learn. Sometimes, we refuse to learn them. But that's us, not Him."

She thought about her failed marriages. It was always so easy to blame the man. He had wandering eyes. He'd been taken in by pretty words and led away by the challenge of something new. Or maybe even tempted by connections. Whether he actually felt a better connection with her, or, after all, her assistant knew a lot of people because of her association with Bellamy Levine. And her ex-husband had wanted to make it big. Maybe he'd seen her assistant, and his relationship with her, as the key to his big breakthrough.

Regardless, she had to stop focusing on what he had done wrong and focus on what she could fix.

"So maybe, getting out of LA was the first thing I could do to not repeat the mistakes of my past. Just talking to you makes it obvious that there really are men of character in the world. Even if I had lost my faith in humanity for a while."

"There are. Maybe you needed to come out here to restore your faith in humanity."

"Maybe. Although I thought I was coming to terms with the idea that marriage wasn't for me."

He shoved a hand in his pocket. His voice was soft. "I don't think God created man nor woman to be alone. Although, sometimes I look around at marriages and see that maybe just because you're married doesn't mean you're not alone."

"I know how that feels." She'd never had someone voice it like that—how it felt to be married to someone who only thought of himself.

He didn't say anything, and somehow it felt safe for her to open her mouth and say, "I was too young when I got married the first time. Neither one of us was ever home. We didn't want to sit around and be thought of as losers by our friends."

"Is it funny that when you're young, staying home seems to be a stigma. But there's really no place I'd ever rather be."

"It's the best place to be. If it has the right spirit. But I wasn't making it a home, and he wasn't interested in having someone who was Susie Homemaker anyway. He wanted arm candy, and I just wanted to get out. Or maybe I wanted someone to love me."

"I think we all want that. Long for that. It's kind of funny, because God does love us, but we reject that, thinking somehow the love of a fellow human is more important."

"But, like you pointed out, God created us to need the fellow human kind of love too or at least to need a companion. Someone to walk beside us, which seems like what marriage should be about."

"Yeah. Instead, it's kind of about making ourselves happy. Because we 'fall in love,' and then we expect the other person to make us happy."

"For never being married, you have a lot of wisdom."

"I don't think I need to be married to see what's going on with other people. Plus, the Bible is full of wisdom. You read it, and then the things around you make sense. Because you start looking at it through the lens of the way God thinks instead of the lens of the way man thinks."

"Interesting. I've never found the Bible an easy book to read."

"Most things worth doing aren't easy."

"Like staying married."

"True. I don't think anyone stands at the altar thinking that it's going to be a hard thing to do. But it ends up that way. At least if you marry someone who isn't as committed as you are. Or who doesn't care about anyone but themselves."

"There are lots of people like that out there. I was married to one of those. That's the only marriage I left."

"Because he didn't pay attention to you?"

"Because he couldn't love anyone but himself. And, looking back, I realize that just because I wasn't getting what I wanted didn't make it okay for me to break my vows. At the time, I listened to everyone who said my needs weren't being met, so I needed to

go find someone else. Someone who could meet my needs. But...
That's a pretty hard responsibility to strap on to someone else
when you get married, 'you have to meet all my needs.'"

"Especially when you consider the reciprocal should also be true.
If I expect my spouse to meet all of my needs, then I need to meet
all of theirs, and...that's impossible."

"Yeah."

"It's like we expect our spouses to do what God is supposed to
do."

"True. To love us like God is supposed to love us, and to meet
our needs when God has already promised to meet our needs. I
guess we're always looking for something or someone to take the
place of God in our lives. Even Christians. We don't even realize
we're doing it. It's what society does, and Christians pick that up.
After all, you're considered odd if you don't accept the general
prevailing wisdom of the day, even if that wisdom isn't wisdom
but foolishness."

"'Thinking themselves to be wise, they became fools.'" She
couldn't believe she'd remembered that verse, but it was one she
had memorized as a child.

"Exactly," he said, sounding kind of impressed and a little surprised.

"You didn't think I knew any Bible."

"Most people don't."

"I'm most people. But that verse just came to me as we were
talking."

"Funny the things God will put in your head, the things you
learned as a child, they come back when you actually have a conversation and think about it. We usually don't think about what the
Bible says though. We want to go to every expert, people who are
looking for every reason not to believe the Bible, and we listen to
them and believe what they say instead."

They were quiet for a while. They'd been talking for a long time,
and while Bellamy wasn't the slightest bit sleepy, it was probably
more than time to go to bed.

"Thanks for not being angry with me about today."

"I can't imagine being angry. I appreciate you watching the boys. Glad no one got hurt. And I'm sorry I'm not going to be able to get your cabin fixed anytime soon."

He'd already told her earlier that the things he had been hoping would work weren't going to. And that they would be stuck in the same cabin together if they both wanted a washer and dryer, toilet and stove and shower. He'd be working on the other cabins, but none of them were made to be lived in for any length of time. Most of them weren't plumbed at all, either.

"It's not your fault. And after what you told me today about the boys, it feels like maybe they do need some love in their life."

"Yeah. They need a mom and a dad and a place where they belong."

She froze. Something about his words made her think that they were kind of like a family here. She was a sorry excuse for a mom, and Calhoun, with his odd ways and his insistence on waiting for God to bring him the right girl, was hardly a candidate for a dad. And she wasn't even sure the boys would know how to relate to a family like that.

But... "Do you believe that everything happens for a reason?" she asked, just because it hit her that somehow God had orchestrated things so that she was here, Calhoun was here, and there were three boys between them.

"I was thinking the same thing."

"Interesting."

"Yeah. I guess... I guess maybe God speaks to us in funny ways."

She wasn't sure exactly what he was saying, but it almost seemed like a reference to their earlier conversation where she was asking how he would know that he had found the right girl, the one that God wanted for him. But...surely he couldn't be. Because he would be implying that she was the one.

And she and Calhoun were worlds apart. So different it wasn't even funny. So not suited for each other.

And Calhoun had not seemed like he looked at her in any kind of romantic way. At all. She thought to herself how they weren't flirting but just having an intellectual conversation.

But Calhoun wasn't like every other man she knew. He didn't insinuate, didn't make suggestive comments, and seemed to be content to allow someone else to pick out his lifetime mate. Even if it was God.

She didn't have a chance to ask him about it because he pushed off from the porch post and said, "Are you going to be okay? I think I'm going to take a walk."

She wouldn't mind going with him. She didn't think she'd be afraid to walk in the unknown darkness with Calhoun beside her. She didn't want to ask, and the invitation had clearly not been for her. He'd wanted her to stay.

"I'll be fine. I'm going to go in and go to bed. I'm hoping tomorrow I'll get a chance to improve upon today. It shouldn't be hard." She meant it as a joke, but he didn't even grunt. Just jerked his head at her and stepped off the porch, walking away with the light of the moon on his back. She didn't really want to, but she ended up watching him anyway. The long stride, the confident angle of his shoulders, the straightness of his back, and the complete ease with which he walked off into the night.

It made her think that maybe she should ask the Lord to let her know what she should do with her life, instead of deciding for herself that she was finished with marriage.

What a novel idea.

Chapter 17

*Making time for each other-date nights & having God as the
center of marriage.
- Terri Voth-Pryor from OK*

Bellamy rolled out of bed a lot earlier than she could ever remember getting up since she'd been in high school. But her conversation with Calhoun the night before had made her think.

She couldn't change the people around her, but she could change herself. Part of that was taking what she'd been given and doing her best with it.

She had been planning on taking time for herself, to find herself, maybe.

But God had placed three boys and a man in her life. Maybe, rather than finding herself, she was better off losing herself and serving them.

The idea had been sparked by Calhoun's words, but as with all ideas, it was up to her to implement.

That's why she'd set her alarm and why she'd gotten out of bed, even though her eyes weren't quite open.

As she came down the stairs, Calhoun sat in the recliner by the window, his Bible open on his lap in front of him, his eyes lifted in concern, then in inquiry. Like somehow he was able to look at her and know she wasn't the type of person who normally got up before the sun.

Way before the sun.

Two of the boys were already up and playing with their new toy trucks at Calhoun's feet.

Calhoun started to shift, but Bellamy put her hand up. "You keep doing what you're doing. If you don't mind, I was going to make breakfast."

Rather than relaxing him, her words made his brows shoot up even further.

"I'm not much of a cook." That seemed to be the question on his face. "But I make really good cinnamon toast. If that's okay, that's what we'll have for breakfast."

He nodded slowly, his brows going back down and what looked like possibly the start of a smile twitching on his lips. "Sounds good."

She nodded, reaching the bottom of the stairs, and then, since he hadn't looked back down at the book in his lap, she added, "If you trust me, I think the boys and I can handle school today."

That caused him to blink and his eyebrows to shift up, although not quite as far.

The rest of his face didn't flinch though, and to his credit, he answered immediately. "I appreciate it, and of course I trust you."

She gave him a smile that said the "of course" probably surpassed the positive thinking point and fell into the fantasy.

He gave her a grin that said he was pretty sure he understood exactly what she was saying.

She hadn't heard him come in the night before and had no idea how long his walk had been. But he didn't seem depressed or upset this morning. In fact, she almost felt like there was a connection between them that hadn't been there before.

It scared her a little, because while their conversation last night had convinced her that swearing off marriage was probably a bad idea, she still wanted to prove that she would be fine without a man. Since her entire adult life had been a seesaw in and out of relationships. She was done with the drama. She wanted a break from it anyway.

Although something told her that there would be no drama with Calhoun.

Not in North Dakota, but maybe another location would be drama. After all, she could hardly be an actress with the home base of North Dakota. Whoever heard of such a thing?

And Calhoun didn't seem like the kind of man who would be happy living in town, let alone in a city like LA.

And wow, she thought as she pulled the bread down, set it on the counter, and opened the bag, how had she gone from feeling a connection to Calhoun to trying to figure out where they would live together?

She shook her head at herself. That was what she was trying to get out of. Always having a man in the picture.

By the time she had ten slices of cinnamon toast ready, Cayson had gotten up, and Calhoun had closed his Bible and started setting the table.

The boys chattered around them, having way too much energy for this early in the morning, and she didn't try to start a conversation with Calhoun as he set plates around. After all, they'd talked a lot last night, and he'd left their conversation rather abruptly.

"You must've slept well, since you're up so early. Or else you didn't sleep," Calhoun said as he moved to pull silverware out of the drawer beside her.

"I slept okay. Although I did a lot of thinking. Do you have that effect on everyone you talk to?" she asked, meaning it mostly as a joke, but his hand paused, and he looked at her.

"And here I thought it was you that was making me think. Do you have that effect on everyone you talk to?" He mimicked her question. Which made her smile. Their eyes caught, and she wondered if he was thinking the same thing she was. She didn't have that effect on anyone. Except, apparently, him.

She didn't need anything else to make her feel like Calhoun was...special. Different. Someone she wouldn't mind getting to know better.

And why not? Hadn't the Lord arranged her life so that they would be spending time together? Why was she so against it?

Then she remembered what he'd said about waiting for the Lord to show him his mate. God certainly wasn't going to pick a girl like her for a man like Calhoun.

His expression changed, almost as though he could see the direction her thoughts were going, but he didn't say anything, turning from the drawer with the knife that he'd pulled from it.

By the time she finished sprinkling cinnamon on the last piece of toast, he had all of the pieces cut in halves and the plate on the table.

He said the blessing, and then as the boys were eating, he laid down some rules for the schooling after he was gone. Bellamy listened, trying not to shake her head in wonder. He'd either figured it out, or maybe the boys had told him, that she lost control because after he'd left, they'd started complaining about their schoolwork and refused to do it.

While Bellamy wanted to be able to control them on her own, she appreciated his support and the fact that he was tying in whether or not they could spend the afternoon helping him to whether or not they cooperated with her in the morning.

She cleared away the dishes and took care of them while he got the boys started on their work. She had just finished wiping the counter when he came over with his phone.

"I wasn't sure whether you had an idea for lunch or not?"

"I assumed I'd cook it since I'd be here, but... I think you probably figured out that my skills are limited."

"Mine were at one time too. Just takes practice." He paused. "So you don't have anything planned for lunch?"

She laughed. "I hadn't gotten over my dread long enough to make a plan."

"If it's a hardship, I don't mind cooking at all. Just let me know, I can stop a little early."

"I feel like it would be a good thing for me to learn. I also feel like it might be a good thing for the kids to learn as well." She didn't add that just in case he didn't retain custody, and just in case they were put in a position where they had to cook for themselves, it might be a good idea for them to learn, but the thought was there.

A look crossed his face that said maybe he had been thinking the same thing, but it disappeared quickly. She was beginning to realize he was a man who didn't dwell on the negative. Not the negative in situations, and not the negative in people. She found out, now that she had been off of social media for more than a day, that her natural inclination was not to dwell on the negative either.

But when faced with the negative on a daily basis, that's where her mind went.

"I have to agree with you." And that's all he said about that. He held up his phone in his hand. "I can text you a link. I have some recipes that have videos to go with them and use ingredients that we have. If you're interested, I'll send them to you, and you can make a decision about what you'd like to make. But I'll have my phone with me all day, although not constantly, and if it's too much, or you have any questions, I'm not going to be far away. Just ask."

It didn't feel too overwhelming when he put it like that. In fact, put like that, where she would have the video, and he was just right outside, not far away at all, ready to answer any questions she had, she felt like she could do it.

"Thanks," she said, wanting to say more but not knowing how to phrase it. He was probably thinking she was a little bit pathetic since she needed so much help. Even if he did say everyone had to start somewhere. After all, he hadn't been born knowing how to cook.

Her phone was upstairs, but it was charged, and it would be just a matter of a few seconds to get it. Somehow, his words had made her more confident, and while she hadn't exactly been dreading the morning, she hadn't been sure that she would be able to handle the things that were put in front of her.

But with Calhoun's last few sentences, she no longer felt like she was doing it on her own.

Maybe this is what a marriage should feel like. That it was no longer just her struggling on her own, but she had a helper.

"I owe you," she said as he started to turn away.

"That's funny. I was thinking it was the other way around. After all, no one told you you had to actually do anything with the boys. Just because you're stuck in this cabin, there is no rule that says you have to watch the kids too."

Of course not. She wasn't figuring for one second that he was expecting her to watch them. She had just decided that that was what God had wanted her to do since that's what He seemed to put in front of her.

"So I figured the least I could do was try to help out a little. Since you're doing something so huge for me."

She smiled and shook her head. "I hadn't even thought about the idea that I was doing it for you. I just had been thinking that I make my plans, and I do what I want, and that's how I live my life. And I fight against anything that gets in my way. But obviously that hasn't worked out for me. And it's kind of obvious that while I had plans for over the holidays, God has changed them. So instead of fighting this time, maybe I ought to just be open to the idea that perhaps He has something else for me to do."

"Something else to learn. There's usually a lesson somewhere, or multiple lessons, if we have our eyes open."

"Exactly. Something else to do, something else to learn, some way I'm supposed to grow. I want to be a better person, but I want it to happen somehow while I'm chasing after things that benefit me. But you don't become a better person by chasing after yourself."

"That's right. You become a better person by losing yourself."

She nodded. It went against everything that modern psychology taught, but it was the truth. A person grew when they stopped catering to themselves and started seeing others.

Calhoun left shortly after, with all three boys sitting at the table, working on their schooling. She was going to have to teach math class, and Calhoun had shown her the lesson for Calvin, who was ahead of the other two boys. But both Cruz and Cayson would be doing the same things. At least until their books came. She also had to listen to them read.

Calhoun had promised to do history and science in the evenings when he was home. But they wouldn't be starting those classes for a bit. He'd grinned and said they'd ease into it.

This wasn't exactly easing into anything; she felt like she was being tried by fire, since she was not only going to have to do homeschooling today but cook a meal for four other people.

Lots of learning curves.

But again, rather than striking fear in her heart, the idea made her smile, and she knew it was all because Calhoun was behind her, completely. That gave her confidence.

"This is too hard," Cayson said, sounding very much like he had the day before, which had been the beginning of her total and complete loss of control.

Asking God to give her strength and wisdom, because after all if this was what He wanted her to do, He needed to somehow equip her to do it, she strode over, setting the math instructions down and looking at the reading that Cayson was doing.

She had no idea how to help.

Use the talent that God has given you. You just said He would equip you. Maybe He already has.

Chapter 18

When both of you realize that marriage isn't 50-50. Both
need to give 100%, all the time.
- Alice Neal from Lewistown, MT

The only talent that Bellamy ever had that was worth anything was her acting skills.

In high school, she could have used them to get out of trouble if her mom had cared at all about her, but she'd been allowed to do pretty much whatever she wanted to anyway and only had to use her acting skills at school on her teachers.

Maybe she could put them to good use now.

She looked at Cayson's story. It was a short story, taken from Aesop's fables, about an animal getting rocks out of a jar.

"How about I read it to you first?" That was the only way she knew how to use her acting skills, and she didn't wait for Cayson to nod but stood at the table beside him, glancing at the story and reading it, using all the inflection she possessed, and allowing her body to naturally move while she used her hands and expressions to tell the story.

It was just a simple two-paragraph story, using mostly one- and two-syllable words, but she gave it everything she had, like it was an audition that her career hinged on. By the time she was done, she'd completely gotten in character and was slightly surprised to look up and see all three boys staring at her with mouths open. Engrossed.

She grinned, a little self-consciously.

"Now you try it, Cayson."

A smile spread across Cayson's face, almost as though her performance had inspired him to do the same.

Indeed, now that he knew what the story was about, the words were a little easier to figure out, and his interest had gone from negative numbers to extremely high.

She could tell because he tried to imitate her inflections, even getting his hands up and moving around and fisting one to show how the fox couldn't get it out of the jar. Just as she had done, he shook it in the air, like there was a jar attached to it.

She felt like that was a win.

And it set the tone for the rest of the morning. She had found that using her skills, her acting skills, made school fun. Fun meant interest, and interest meant learning. Maybe it was an accidental discovery, but everything she said, everything she did, she tried to look at it through the lens of her acting skills, and she ended up acting out math problems and answers and even getting all of the boys up and using them as objects in a word problem.

By the time it was time for her to quit and start on lunch, Calvin said, "I hated word problems, but they were fun today."

Those simple words made her soul sing the same way a good review that praised her acting talent might have. After all, it was a testament to her acting skills that his eyes had been opened and he'd seen math word problems in a new way.

Everything wasn't roses. They hadn't gotten all of their work done. They spent a lot more time talking about it and acting it out rather than doing it, and she'd been a little stumped on multiplication since she hadn't had enough people to help Calvin learn his facts. But she supposed if she put her mind to it, she could figure something out.

Maybe she could tell stories about his multiplication facts. Make up stories about the numbers.

She wasn't a bad artist. Maybe tonight when Calhoun had taken over, she could work on drawing some pictures and making up stories to make the math facts stick.

That's what she was thinking about as she ran upstairs to grab her phone so she could get the text that Calhoun had sent her with the link for lunch.

Smiling as she grabbed it, she glanced down, intending only to unplug it and run back out of her room, but a familiar name came up on her screen.

Houston Park.

I'm sorry. We make such a great team. Give me another chance?

She was over him. So over him. But she still couldn't help the emotional reaction she felt when she saw his text. He was actually apologizing.

She couldn't believe it. He was sorry? He was admitting that he had done something wrong? That it wasn't just her not being a good wife or whatever other accusations he had thrown at her when he had insisted that she had driven him to her assistant, rather than him cheating on her with her assistant. He'd never placed an ounce of blame on Wanda, either. It was always Bellamy.

Then she stopped herself.

Stop being so gullible. You know what he's like.

On a hunch, she opened up the web browser, because she'd deleted all her apps, and pulled up the first social media site she thought of.

Sure enough, all the hype was about how successful their movie had been.

She supposed if she opened up her email, she'd find messages from her agent, even though her agent had been told not to disturb her, asking if she was interested in taking a look at the offers that she'd been sent.

Wishing she could just drop the phone and leave it in her room, but knowing she couldn't cook lunch without it, she clasped it in her hand, holding it to her side after closing her web browser and going down the stairs a lot more slowly than she came up them.

"What's wrong with you?" Calvin asked as he looked up from finishing his last math problems.

It must be pretty bad if the boys could notice a change in her demeanor.

Funny how just a few words, just a few pictures, just a few thoughts could totally change her mood.

Had social media ever changed her for the better?

Holding her phone up, she ignored Calvin for the moment, and did something she should have done after the premier this summer, and blocked Houston Park's number. She deleted their conversation.

Whatever happened, she didn't want to be sucked into going online again.

She had a purpose, these three boys, and whatever wisdom God wanted her to learn from Calhoun, and she needed to focus on that right now. Not be sidetracked by things that didn't matter.

"I'm sorry that I look unhappy," she said, putting a smile on her face that almost felt natural, as she walked over to Calvin, looking at the problems on his paper.

"You looked angry."

"And scary," Cayson added, in a voice that sounded far less sure than anything else he'd said in the last couple of hours.

"Like someone did something bad and you want to spank them," Cruz added, just in case she hadn't figured out exactly how she looked from everyone else.

"Well, that's very helpful, boys. Thank you for making sure I know exactly how I look." She gave them a cheesy grin. "Do I look like I want to kill anyone now?"

"Maybe." Cruz wrinkled his nose.

Cayson nodded slowly, like he was agreeing with Cruz.

"You look like you're thinking about it but don't want anyone to know."

She put her hands on her hips and looked at the boys with her head down like she was looking over her nose and a pair of schoolmarm glasses, and gave them all her best schoolmarm look.

"I think you boys are teasing me. I think I looked extremely happy, so happy that you all just couldn't stand it, so you had to make up all that other stuff about me looking like I'm thinking like I'm going to murder people, when you all know that I absolutely would never ever do anything of the sort." She somehow managed to inflict her voice with the schoolmarm sound and still make it sound like she absolutely would murder people without a second thought, like she did it all the time. But she did it with a twist of humor that had the boys all laughing.

She figured, since their schoolwork was mostly done, there was no harm in being a little goofy, right?

She dropped the schoolmarm look, laughed along with them, and then said, "All right, who's helping with lunch today?"

All three boys jumped up screaming that they wanted to do it.

Maybe they could set up a schedule later, but since she asked, and they'd all volunteered, she hated to not let them all help, so she said, "All right. I know nothing about cooking. I'm not even sure I can turn on the stove, since it's a gas stove and I've never used one of those before." Calhoun had turned it on for her last night when she warmed up the canned soup.

"It's easy. I'll show you how," Calvin said confidently, setting his pencil down and standing up.

"How many houses have you exploded by turning on the stove?" she asked, her tone so serious it actually made Calvin's head snap around and his mouth hang open before he saw the twinkle in her eye.

"None." He sounded defensive, but he was also smiling.

"All right. We're tied. This is a competition where the person with the highest number loses, just wanted to throw that out there," she said, just in case he thought the goal was to explode the house. Goodness. That would probably qualify her for the worst cook of the year award.

Not an award she had any ambitions toward winning. Although it kind of sounded like an award that would fit her.

By the time Calhoun had come in half an hour later, they hadn't even gotten to the turning on the stove part. They'd watched the video three or four times, gotten all the ingredients out, and Bellamy had finally figured out where the mixing bowls were. They looked all through the kitchen, since there wasn't much cabinet or counter space, but she finally figured out there were cupboards underneath the island, and that was where the bowls were.

She was standing up with the bowls in her hand, holding them triumphantly over her head like a trophy and calling out, "I found them! I found them! We need to celebrate!"

Her eyes met Calhoun's as he stood in the doorway.

Memories of the day before, when she'd been standing at the edge of the ledge, holding onto the four corners of her bedsheet and getting ready to jump as he walked in, seemed to float in the air between them.

He didn't say anything but shut the door without taking his eyes off her.

"Maybe you could try to walk in sometime when I'm not acting like an idiot. It would help with my confidence," she said, like helping with her confidence was his goal in life or something.

"I'll keep that in mind. Maybe you could, oh, you know, text me when you're not acting like an idiot."

The boys laughed, and she did too.

"You might be waiting for a while for that text," she said, looking around at the boys, who were laughing and agreeing with her.

"So what happened today? Or don't I want to know?" Calhoun's eyes swept the four of them, as though he were looking for broken bones or signs that anyone had been jumping off of the furniture or the stairs. "No one was learning how to fly today?"

"We study the Wright brothers tomorrow," Bellamy said in her new schoolmarm voice.

"Let's skip that lesson," Calhoun said immediately.

"Who are the Wright brothers?" Calvin asked.

"Can we learn about them today?" Cruz said.

"Yeah! Please?"

"Will you act that out?" Cayson asked, which didn't wipe the smile off of Calhoun's face, but it did make his eyes narrow suspiciously.

"Sounds like things went well today?" he said slowly, ending it like a question.

"Miss Bellamy made school fun," Calvin said and then launched into how she had turned his math problems into actual stories, and acted them out, and how it made it easier for him to understand,

and how he was able to do it, and she even made people laugh over his math story problems.

Calhoun listened with half grin on his face, intently, although every once in a while, his eyes would lift, and he'd look at Bellamy, who shrugged a little, grinning as she listened to Calvin describe their day. It was even better than she had imagined, although it was definitely from his point of view. She loved how seeing herself through his eyes gave her ideas to do things differently, better, the next day. She was looking forward to it, to her great surprise.

It took about fifteen minutes for all the boys to tell Calhoun everything about their morning, and in the meantime, Bellamy watched the video one more time, getting the chicken out and starting drying it like it showed in the steps.

Calhoun had the boys cleaning the table and setting it when he walked over to the counter.

"I'm impressed. It sounds like everyone had a great time today. You even look happy."

"I had fun!"

"Glad to hear it. When a kid can tell me what they learned in school, that means he really learned it. And I wasn't having to drag it out of them, they couldn't wait to tell me. That's impressive."

Her heart swelled under his praise. Feeling her chest was floating, she quit patting the chicken and turned to him.

"I needed the conversation we had last night. I just needed to see that the direction that I needed to go was in the direction that God wants me to go. And I always heard God doesn't give us anything we can't handle, so I just asked Him to help me. And that's when I got my answer. I was already equipped. He wanted me to use the skills that He'd given me to do the job He had in front of me."

She shrugged her shoulders and held up one hand, careful to keep from waving the knife in Calhoun's face. They were joking about her killing people, but she didn't want to actually hurt any-one. "It all kind of fell into place. He actually has already equipped me for the job He gave me. It's kind of unbelievable."

"Yeah." He agreed with her, but his answer seemed a little pre-occupied too, and that's when she realized he was watching her, his eyes going over her face, seeming to see her excitement and be...impressed? No, attracted. It was attractive to him.

That made her heart beat faster, and heat crept up her neck.

The boys weren't the only thing that God placed in front of her.

But he was waiting for the right girl. And she'd already decided God would never think that was her.

Why wouldn't He? Why else would He have her here?

Calhoun didn't say anything for a while, and they just looked at each other, her words fleeing, as she looked at the expression on his face, wondering what it meant.

"Thanks," he finally said. Then, he seemed to shake himself. "Let me give you a hand with this."

"The boys are supposed to be helping me. They all wanted to, but I had trouble finding all the things, since I didn't know my way around the kitchen. That's what we were celebrating when you came in. I hadn't realized there was a cupboard underneath the island, and I found the mixing bowls." She was rambling but couldn't seem to stop herself.

"That's worth celebrating," he said, and it didn't seem like he was being condescending or patronizing her. Rather, they were just laughing together. "Are you going to give us all jobs?"

She laughed. "I don't even know what I'm doing, let alone be able to delegate. How about you do that, and I'll just do what you tell me to since you're here."

He grunted and glanced at the recipe. "You're making Jenna's Favorite Chicken. I love that one."

"Who's Jenna?" Cruz asked, coming over and standing between them.

Bellamy just stared at him, not expecting that question.

"It's probably a young girl who has a dad who loves her and named his chicken recipe after her," Calhoun said, not seeming fazed by his question.

"I want a recipe named after me!" Cruz exclaimed.

"We can change the name of this one," Bellamy suggested, taking the package of bacon that Calhoun handed her.

"But, if we do, it won't be special for Jenna anymore." Calvin stood by the table, his eyes sad for the unknown Jenna. Like changing the name of the recipe would be taking something from her, even though she wouldn't even know it.

"I guess we don't want to do that." Calhoun paused as he set a can of tomatoes on the counter. "I'm sure Jenna is just as special to her dad as you are to me."

Bellamy picked up the can opener along with the tomatoes, watching the boys while pretending to be focused on opening the can. She wanted to meet Calhoun's gaze, because she'd been impressed with how Calvin had been concerned about Jenna's feelings, even though he didn't even know her – didn't even know if she were real.

"But I want a recipe named after me!" Cruz insisted, like the benchmark for him knowing that he was loved and wanted was to have food named after him.

Bellamy bit her lip, trying to figure out how to solve this puzzle – keep Jenna's name for Calvin, but give Cruz a food for himself.

"Let me see," Calhoun said in a normal tone as he picked up his phone and looked at it. "We're making Jenna's Favorite Chicken for the crockpot for tonight, but we're making William's sausage pasta for right now. I suppose we don't want to change the name of William's pasta because his dad probably named it after him and he might feel left out?"

All three boys stood looking at Calhoun and all three nodded their heads, although Cruz wasn't quite as firm in his nodding as the other two, since he seemed a little torn about still wanting something named after himself.

Calhoun tapped a finger on his phone.

Bellamy set the can down on the counter along with the can opener. "I have an idea."

The boys looked at her.

"You know the cinnamon toast I made for breakfast this morning?"

They nodded.

"That's my recipe, but I haven't named it. We could call it Cruz's Cinnamon Toast."

"Yeah!" Cruz said immediately. Then, almost as though a thought had hit his brain with enough force to close his mouth, he said, "But...what about Calvin and Cayson? They need recipes, too."

"That's really big of you to think of them," Calhoun said and ruffled Cruz's hair. He glanced at Bellamy. "We could call it The Three C's Cinnamon Toast."

She shook her head right away. "It would have to be The FOUR C's Cinnamon Toast."

The boys took a minute to digest that.

"But that doesn't include you," Calvin finally said.

"How about B's Four C's Cinnamon Toast?" Calhoun's eyes sparkled as his eyes met Bellamy's. Something warm and happy settled in her chest. It had been growing there all morning but had gotten stronger as they'd started working together in the kitchen. Like a real family, even though they were anything but.

"That's perfect!" Calvin shouted, truly excited for the first time.

"Yeah! That includes the whole family," Cruz said, his face beaming.

Bellamy's eyes got big, and she looked again at Calhoun, who, for once, seemed at a loss as to how to respond. She knew he wanted to keep the boys. Knew he considered them a gift from God to him, but...she wasn't a part of that.

Still, he didn't seem upset, and, in fact, as she watched, his face lightened, almost as though something had clicked into place for him.

"Sure does," he said to Cruz, putting his arm around Cayson, who had sidled up next to him and wrapped one arm around his waist.

Calvin stared at the way Calhoun was hugging Cayson. There was a longing his eye that made Bellamy's heart feel like it wanted to cry. She moved her arm, stretching it out. Calvin's eye caught the movement and he turned toward her, looking at her arm and the open circle it made. He hesitated for a heartbeat, then grabbed Cayson with one hand and stepped into the circle of Bellamy's arms, hugging her along with his little brother.

She pulled both lips in and squeezed the boys as close as she dared, her chest feeling so big and tight and full she could hardly breathe. Or maybe that was because of her throat closing and her eyes burning with tears that she didn't want to cry, because she didn't want to have to explain to the boys how much she hurt for them but loved them at the same time and how much they'd made her feel needed and useful and like she'd found her purpose in life, even if that purpose wasn't going to be an easy road. Not even a little.

At that thought, she lifted her head and found Calhoun staring at her. It was hard for her to tell, but she thought he was feeling a lot of the same things she was. She saw his throat work and thought maybe his eyes were a bit misty, too.

She wasn't sure how long they stood there in the kitchen like that, but finally the boys seemed to get a little restless, and Calhoun cleared his throat.

"Alright, enough of the mushy stuff. Let's get moving on William's sausage and Jenna's chicken before we all starve to death."

That elicited some giggles out of the boys and made Bellamy smile, too, breaking the heaviness that had descended into her soul.

The five of them made lunch together and had Jenna's Favorite Chicken in the slow cooker for supper and were sitting at the table ready to eat by noon.

There had been a lot of laughing and a lot of mess, but the fun they had was worth it.

What really made it special were the times where she met Calhoun's gaze over the heads of boys, and they shared their own secret looks. Smiles, amusement, and...maybe something else. She wasn't sure exactly what, but whatever it was, she loved the feeling of having someone, someone like a partner. And even though maybe she was doing something that was serving others, it didn't feel like she was serving. It felt like they were all having fun together.

Maybe that's how it felt when she did it right.

Chapter 19

*Don't let the small stuff build into a huge problem and keep
the Lord as the head of your household.*
- Diane Wagner

A week later, they were sitting in the living room in the evening which had become the custom. They did science after the table was cleared. Then they moved to the living room to do history.

For the first few nights, Calhoun had done everything, starting with the story he told, and then they talked about it after he was finished, but the boys had begged for Bellamy to tell the story.

Calhoun had to admit Bellamy didn't just tell the story. She acted it out, making it seem like it was almost real.

He could see why she had a successful acting career. Not only was she beautiful, but she had the talent to go with the looks.

Calhoun had been equal parts happy and discouraged.

Happy because Bellamy had obviously found her niche, and the boys loved her, and that definitely was worth being thankful for.

The discouragement came because the idea that she might be content in a small North Dakota town was obviously out of the question. She had been born for bigger things.

As much as he tried convincing himself of this, his heart wasn't listening.

After all, maybe rather than waiting for a woman who was *waiting* for him, maybe he'd been waiting for a woman who was *ready* for him.

He found that as long as her past didn't have a hold of her, and it didn't seem to, he didn't care about it.

She hadn't seemed interested in him, but maybe he'd misjudged that too. He'd heard that people who were falling in love often did think with their emotions rather than their intellect.

As he stared across the living room at her, the flickering candlelight bathing her face in a soft glow, romantic even, although he'd never been into that kind of thing, he found he could see the benefits.

Although, he supposed that having three boys spread around, asking questions and making comments, wasn't the most romantic thing ever.

But it felt right. Warm, honest, cozy like...a family.

He studied her face as she talked. Maybe he was the only one feeling those things, and she couldn't wait to leave. But she hadn't asked him one time about her cabin or when it would be ready, and she seemed content with the boys and the homeschooling and spending the afternoons helping him with whatever he was working on.

Most of the time, Bellamy was right beside him, with the boys doing what they could.

They came home, made supper together, and spent the evening finishing school.

Usually they got done in time to play a couple games, unless the boys really got caught up in the lesson, and they ended up talking about it more, sometimes even acting more stories out.

Bellamy yawned. "I think we talked right through our game time today. You guys really like the Revolutionary War."

"I like the idea of not letting bullies get away with things," Calvin said, his chest puffed out a little because, while they told the facts as they were, good and bad, he was proud of his country.

A good thing for a citizen to feel. An important thing for a citizen to feel. Because a country was built on the foundation that had been laid before their time. And while their country was imperfect, they'd been given a solid foundation, one based on Christian principles and morals and values. Not on greed, or caste systems, or government strength. But rather on individual freedoms.

They were helping the boys feel like, no matter what their past was, they could achieve anything they wanted to, because that's how their country was set up.

Over their heads, he met Bellamy's eyes and they smiled together.

"You fellas go brush your teeth, and I'll be in to listen to your prayers and say good night," he said, straightening up from his comfortable position in the recliner.

The boys didn't protest. They'd learned it did no good, and he made their bedtime half an hour earlier the next night. They got up and filed out.

Bellamy clicked and swiped a little on her phone, since that was where they'd been getting their stories, since they hadn't picked up any textbooks, before she looked up at him.

He'd been waiting on that because he wanted to talk to her without the boys around.

"I've been hearing that there's a big storm coming."

"Oh?"

He hadn't figured she had heard. The people she talked to in California wouldn't care about the weather in North Dakota, but his dad and brothers had been checking on him occasionally, and even more today, since the storm was supposed to hit the day after tomorrow.

"I think we probably should make a trip to town, stock up on some essentials. They're calling for a couple of feet, but you never know."

"Never know whether it's going to be more or less?"

"Either. Both." He grinned. Sometimes they weren't even right about whether or not they were going to get a storm. But being it was only two days away, it was probably worth the trip to town.

She laughed a little. He smiled. They'd grown comfortable together. He'd almost term them friends. They definitely both had the interest of the children at heart, and after their talk on the porch a week ago, they didn't seem to have any trouble talking to each other.

They'd never gone that deep again though.

"Are you saying you're leaving me here with the boys?"

"I thought maybe you guys would want to come along. Although you don't have to." He knew she might want to get away, and most people didn't mind a trip to town once in a while. Women, as he understood them, liked to go more.

She chewed on her lip, and he didn't really even fight himself to not look at it, just allowed his eyes to rest on the most interesting thing in the room.

"I'd like to go. It kind of surprises me."

"That you want to get out?"

She nodded. "When I came here, I didn't care if I ever saw people again. But... It hasn't been what I expected, and I feel like it's been healing."

"Sometimes just getting your mind off yourself and onto somebody else is all you really need."

She nodded, a little grin on her face. "I guess that's not really something I've ever heard in my life before, but it's true."

"Well, think hard about it, because your latest movie has been playing at the Sweet Water theater. I think people would have recognized you before this, but I've heard it's been popular, and you might be swamped by fans, even in our sleepy town."

"I hardly think that people would recognize me now and wouldn't have before." She lifted her shoulders. "But if you say so."

"Maybe you're right. I guess I don't know anything about it." And that made him sad. He really didn't know anything about her life.

"You've been teaching me about North Dakota, and about building, and homeschooling, and cooking." They exchanged a smile over that last one. She still didn't turn the stove on without stretching an arm out and turning her face away, just in case it exploded. Although, once it was on, she really was getting better at being able to follow directions without needing him beside her every second.

"So you're going to teach me about movies?" he asked, not sure where she was going with what she had started.

"I guess. Or maybe...being famous, if I can say that without conceit."

"Of course you can. It's fact. Most of the country knows who you are. I mean, if Sweet Water knows who you are, there's a good chance the rest of America has already figured it out."

"That's just it. They don't even know who I am. They just know my face."

"Sweet Water will not be content to just know your face. They're going to want to know all of your business too."

"Are they... Will they have a problem with me staying here with you?"

He opened his mouth, then paused. There were still people who had values and morals and didn't believe it was right for an unmarried man to stay with a woman he wasn't married to.

He didn't believe it was right.

And yet... The reality of what they were doing wasn't like that at all. But no one else would know it.

"I guess my biggest thing is not worrying about what the town thinks, necessarily, but it's more not wanting to set a bad example for the children."

"By living together?"

He lifted his shoulder. "They know there's nothing going on between us, although I kind of feel like they might be a little bit young to have the discernment of knowing the difference of nothing going on and something immoral happening."

"I see what you say. Children are usually very focused on them-selves."

"Yeah. Some of us never grow out of that."

She laughed along with him, just a chuckle, because it was prob-ably more sad than funny. Although very true.

"But to answer your question, I assume you're asking if people will be unkind to us because we're living in sin or whatever. I don't think so." There might be an outlier. But he didn't think there would be any big issue. At least, he didn't think so. Mostly because of the reputation he had.

"Are you sure?"

"Mostly. I guess I just have a reputation of not being that kind of person. If I say that there's a reason for us to be living together, be-cause of your cabin, people are going to believe that. Just because that's the reputation I have." He honestly really didn't care. God was the one whose opinion was important. The only thing was, since the boys were in his care, he wanted to give them a good moral example.

"My bad reputation won't wipe out your good one?"

He stood. He didn't like the way she said that. "I don't care. Not about your reputation, not about what it's going to do to mine. I think you, as a person, are more important than that, and I think God knows what we're doing, and that's more important than what people in the town think."

She'd risen with him, her face twisted a little with a derisive look, but it had slowly straightened as he spoke. "You almost have me believing you really think that."

"Because I do." He'd heard the toilet flush several times, and the boys chattering in the bathroom and hall as they went to their beds. They were probably ready for him to go in.

But he didn't want to move.

Didn't want to leave Bellamy.

There was something magnetic about her, something that pulled him in. Pulled his thoughts, pulled his eyes, pulled his whole body and soul.

He took one step closer and put a hand on her cheek. She allowed it, lifting her head to meet his eyes, her own a little confused, a little eager, a little...admiring? Maybe.

"I find myself caring more and more about what you think. How you feel. Maybe I shouldn't."

"Why not?" she whispered softly.

He didn't answer.

"Is it because of the vow you made? The one where you're waiting for the right girl?" She sounded disappointed.

He lifted his shoulder, not wanting to answer that. After all, the feeling that he'd already found the right girl had been growing stronger over the last week, but normal people didn't operate like that. They dated for months, years even, before they decided they were with the right person. They didn't decide anything in a week.

"I can leave."

"No!"

She blinked. Maybe not expecting the vehemence in his tone.

He tried to modulate his voice and search for words that would not scare her away but would still be honest, since he didn't necessarily want to hide his feelings, and he definitely didn't want to lie about them, but again, he didn't want to scare her.

"I know I told you I was waiting for the right girl. That I'd vowed to God I would. And I explained that I didn't want to get my feelings involved before I was sure what God wanted. I still feel that way." He took a breath, sliding his hand from her cheek, touching her arm, and smiling when her fingers entwined with his. "Sometimes I can be a little dense. I get my mind set on waiting, and I don't have my eyes opened to what's in front of me. I got to thinking after we talked that maybe God had to hit me on the head pretty hard. After all, He dropped the perfect woman literally in my house."

"The perfect woman? You're talking about me?"

"You're the only one in my house."

"Did you miss the part where I've been divorced five times? Where I've had more failed relationships than you've had interactions with girls, most likely."

"Sorry." He knew there was a rather large segment of society that felt like experience in romantic matters made a man manly. He hadn't been raised that way, not even close, but he just realized she probably had.

She probably didn't view his lack of experience as a good thing, the way someone in his circles might have. She viewed it as a negative.

"You don't need to apologize. I... I admire that."

"It hadn't occurred to me until just now it was probably something you didn't admire."

"I know people who think it's a bad thing, and maybe at one time, I might have agreed. But at this point in my life, I think it shows character. Integrity. Because rather than running around making yourself feel good, you've been allowing God to have control of your life. That's not an easy thing."

He grunted, because it definitely wasn't an easy thing.

"Do you really think that God put us together for a reason?" she finally asked after long moments of silence, and he wasn't sure whether her expression was disbelief because she wanted it or disbelief because the idea was so preposterous.

"I've never had a peace about something like this before. I'd always joked around when I was talking to the Lord that He was going to have to be very obvious about the girl when He brought her in my life, because I'm dense. I guess I don't know how much more obvious He can be." He paused. "But I want those three boys. I'm gonna fight for them. So… Maybe I'm not a good bet right now."

"Because you want to be a father?"

"Not because of that necessarily, but because… Because I'm gonna come with three kids if I have any say in it." He lifted his shoulder. "I've never really paid attention to women with children. I just assumed God would have a woman who'd been waiting for me like I've been waiting for her."

"I definitely haven't been waiting," she said, discouragement back in her voice.

"Maybe you have. Or maybe, you haven't been ready until now."

He lifted his brows, hoping for her to lift her eyes and meet his gaze again, which she did after a few moments of his silence.

"You say that almost like it's a possibility. That God might actually have meant for us to meet here. Because we were meant to be."

"I've been thinking along those lines. I definitely like you a lot."

"We're so different."

"I know." He swallowed. "But there's no biblical reason why people have to be the same, or even close to being the same, in order to be together."

"God doesn't have rules for that kind of thing?" she asked, her tone implying that God had rules for everything else.

"No. He doesn't. The only rules He has are once you make a vow, and become one before God, no breaking it."

"I have a pretty bad track record in that area."

"I don't." He didn't want to rub it in, but he wanted her to know that he was the kind of person who said he was going to do something and didn't change his mind. He thought that maybe she was that kind of person now, too.

"That might be hard for me. I feel like we're not equal in that area."

"I don't think we're equal in any area. Isn't that a good thing?"

Her brows furrowed. "No? I don't want to come into a relationship thinking that I'm not good enough."

"No one said you weren't good enough. We're just different. Good at different things. I'm good at building houses, you're good at telling the kids stories. I'm good at cooking, you're good at organizing things."

"You're good at waiting on what God wants you to do, I'm good at running ahead and messing everything up."

"Are you telling me you haven't learned anything from all of those mistakes?"

"I've learned a lot." Her words were filled with conviction.

"Then maybe you know more about it than I do. Because I haven't had any of those lessons."

Her fingers tightened on his, momentarily. Like his words had surprised her, but it was obvious from the expression on her face she was thinking about it.

"I need to go put the boys down. Think about it. And I think we'll leave early for town and be back by early afternoon. That way I still have half a day to work, and just in case the storm starts early, we'll be ready."

"That sounds good. I'll plan on going."

Chapter 20

Love, respect of each other's individuality, ready for compro-mises.
- Ana from Macedonia

"I had a feeling when that lady showed up with those three kids that something was about to happen." Nolt set his wrench down and turned to face Calhoun more fully.

They were out in the parking lot of the garage, just the two of them, and Calhoun, wanting a little advice from someone older and wiser but not wanting to drag his dad into it, had stopped to talk to his older brother.

"Just something?"

"Yeah." Nolt crossed his arms over his chest and leaned against the front steer. "I thought at first that it might be that woman, Maci. The kids' mother. But I kind of felt like God wasn't going to give you children without sending someone along to help you take care of them. Just a feeling."

The fact that Nolt was even talking about feelings was odd in itself, but the idea that he had been thinking that the Lord was going to send someone and Calhoun had come to that same conclusion was even more unbelievable. But then a thought hit him.

"Is that why you volunteered to take them?" They'd never actually talked about it. Nolt had never said he wanted a relationship or even hinted at such a thing. Nolt, being a typical brother, was all about protecting his younger brothers and taking care of them. But he played his own personal life close to the vest.

He was already shaking his head, though, before the question was completely out of Calhoun's mouth. "No. It was exactly what I said. And what you said too. They reminded me of us. It hurts, probably for the rest of your life, when your mother doesn't want you."

Calhoun jerked his head. But the idea had gotten him to thinking.

"So why aren't you married?"

He just asked the question straight out. No point beating around the bush, hinting. Because Nolt would brush him off. He might flat-out refuse to answer a direct question. Maybe he would.

But Nolt's eyes dropped to the ground, and he seemed to find the toe of his work boot extremely interesting as it crossed over his other foot. He didn't move.

Finally he said, "She chose someone else."

Simple, but more than Calhoun had ever known. He didn't even know there was a girl.

"Last time I looked, there were a couple of billion women in the world. Just because one chose someone else doesn't mean there aren't several billion still to pick from."

"Pick? Like I choose her and that's the end of it." Nolt grinned a little, deflecting the question.

"You know what I meant."

"And I guess you know what I mean," Nolt finally said, shifting, dropping his arms, and straightening. That probably indicated the conversation was over, but Calhoun didn't move.

"You gonna be stuck on her for the rest of your life?"

"You say that like it's a bad thing."

"It is. When she's unavailable."

He lifted his shoulders. "I just see it as the way I am. The way most of us are. I find one. That's it. Not interested in anyone else."

It didn't matter that they hadn't exchanged vows or rings or anything. Calhoun supposed men like that were actually few and far between. People like that. People who were loyal, dedicated, and didn't hop from one person to another.

Nolt was nothing if not loyal and dedicated.

"That's sad, man," Calhoun finally said.

"Up until last week, you were in the same boat."

"Not really. I didn't have someone I was so stuck on I couldn't lift my eyes to see anyone else."

"You couldn't lift your eyes to see anyone, because you were so busy waiting on the right one. And I'm guessing you had some preconceived notions about what that right one was going to be like."

Calhoun grinned, because Nolt was right. "It's funny, but those five marriages don't scare me in the least. Somehow I feel like they should."

"It's been kind of hard to avoid hearing about her, and from what I understand, three of those marriages were terminated because of adultery. One was because the guy was a complete jerk. And I think one was basically an accident."

Calhoun nodded. That's what he'd figured out.

"I bet she's learned some things. As long as she hasn't learned that divorce is the easy way out, I think you're good."

"I think she's learned the exact opposite. That was why she was here."

Nolt jerked his head. "Figures."

Calhoun figured that was Nolt's way of giving him a blessing.

He hadn't put up any red flags and actually encouraged him in the direction he had been wanting to go. Even though it felt like that was what the Lord wanted, he figured it never hurt to ask around and make sure he wasn't just putting what he wanted in a pretty package and saying it was what God wanted, too.

They talked about a few other things before Calhoun got back in his truck and headed back toward town, stopping at the barbershop where Bellamy had taken the three boys to get haircuts.

They walked down the street together, toward the church, where the Piece Makers had asked him to stop because they'd made quilts for the three boys.

"They meet in a church?" Bellamy asked as they went around the back, going to the basement door.

"They do. I suppose they're loosely tied to it, although you don't have to be a member of the church in order to be a member of the

Piece Makers. At least, I don't think so. I guess I've never really dug into it, since it didn't seem like a group I wanted to join."

Bellamy laughed as he opened the door, and she and the boys walked in.

"We've been waiting on you!" Charlene said, walking forward, her blue hair looking like a steel gray in the dim basement light. They didn't have the harsh fluorescent overhead lights on.

"We had the boys' ears lowered, and Calhoun stopped to see his family," Bellamy said, returning Charlene's hug.

They acted like they knew each other, and Calhoun remembered that the Piece Makers had been there setting out some welcome gifts at the cabin she ended up not staying in.

As he was thinking, his eyes went to the corner where Teresa sat. A quilt on her lap, her hands busy, her eyes down.

It's the quiet ones you have to watch.

At the same time that thought went through his head, he recalled that Teresa's husband had been a handyman, somewhat like Calhoun was. A builder who could also do electrical and plumbing work.

As his eyes caught on her, and those thoughts ran through his head, she lifted her head as though she felt his gaze.

Her head snapped back down immediately, but her hands stilled, and he could see her throat work.

She bit her lips, pulling both of them in her mouth, as her hands, gnarled and wrinkled, lay on the material in her lap.

Then, almost as though she were making a decision, her back straightened, and she deliberately lifted the project off her lap and set it aside, standing and meeting his eyes head-on.

"I need to talk to you," she said, interrupting whatever Charlene had been saying, along with the chatter of the children.

"Teresa. Not yet," Vicki said, concern in her eyes, as they skittered from Teresa to Calhoun to Bellamy. "Give it a few more weeks."

"I can't sleep at night. I've never done anything like this before. I have to say something."

Calhoun wanted to reassure her, but the suspicion that had just taken root in his mind wasn't quite fully formed, so he didn't say anything when Teresa took a hold of his elbow and said, "Would you follow me, please?"

He jerked his head and allowed her to lead him away, down the narrow hallway, where she turned the corner where they couldn't be seen and then said in a low voice, "I vandalized the cabin."

Her words didn't shock him entirely, but several heartbeats passed before he said, "Bellamy's cabin?"

Teresa nodded. "I didn't do all the work myself, but I knew exactly what to do in order to create the most damage. I also knew which parts would be difficult to order in."

"Is that what you ladies were doing when Bellamy showed up at her cabin the first time?" he asked, because while he hadn't found it odd that there was a welcoming committee—after all, it was Sweet Water, and that's what the town did—he had found it strange that they had been there to greet a stranger rather than just dropping off their stuff.

He figured they had probably taken longer than they had estimated in order to do the work they did.

"Yes. We didn't expect to see her, but I'm the only one who has any experience in what we were doing, and…just, it's all on me."

"It's not. It was my idea," Charlene said from the opening in the hall.

"And mine," Kathy said, coming to stand beside Charlene.

"I had something to do with it, too," Vicki said.

As Teresa looked at her three friends, some of the lines in her forehead disappeared.

Calhoun could understand that. It was always easier to face things if a person had his friends at his back.

"I don't understand why. I mean, are you guys, like, turning criminal?" It was the only thing he could think of.

"We were just trying to set you up. You need to get married." That came from Charlene. She was the least shy of the group and the one who was most likely to talk about anything.

"Set me up?"

"With Bellamy. If she didn't have a place to stay, she'd have to stay at your cabin with you. We figured no woman could resist your charms when she was stuck with you for a while."

"My charms?" he said doubtfully. No one had ever told him he was charming. He wasn't sure it was a compliment. After all, charming almost was the same thing as fake. And that was something he was sure he wasn't.

"Sure. Your smoldering looks. Your integrity. Your honesty. Your determination to do right. What woman could resist?"

"There's been a lot of women over the years who could resist," he couldn't help but say, his lips tilting up. It was nice to know that the ladies thought so much of him, but the things they'd mentioned weren't exactly sexy things, things that drew a woman's eye. Not that he knew what those kinds of things were. Probably charm.

But as soon as he thought that, he figured charm might draw a woman's eye, but if there was no substance under it, she would leave.

Maybe the substance didn't draw eyes, and maybe that's why the women thought that he needed to be stuck with someone. Because his assets were assets that a person appreciated over time.

"Do I owe you guys a thank you?" he said uncertainly.

"I don't know. Do you?" Charlene asked, her head tilted.

"I don't know. That's why I was asking."

"Did it work? Did our scheme get you guys together? I mean after all, you're here together, and she's kind of looking at you like she likes you."

"She's looking at him like he invented the telephone," Kathy said, her voice low and teasing.

"If that was romantic, I missed it," Calhoun said, mostly joking. Because, after all, what did the telephone have to do with romance?

"Are you two together?" Charlene asked point-blank.

Chapter 21

Compromise, Thoughtfulness, Understanding.
- Verna Westman from Rochester, Washington

Calhoun closed his mouth and looked up at the cobwebs in the far corner. He didn't know how to answer that question, and he didn't want to anyway. After all, Bellamy knew he was interested, but they hadn't talked about the future at all. How his life might be able to merge with hers. What they would do about the boys. What her plans were after the holidays. What he would do for a living, which had to be taken care of, since now that he had three boys. What was he going to do with them while he worked at the garage?

"It might be a possibility, if she'll have me." He spoke, knowing there really wasn't a good answer.

"I'll have him." Bellamy's voice came down the hall, clear and confident. He turned.

She was looking straight at him, her brows lifted almost in a challenge, although she looked every inch the movie star, straight, slim, and beautiful.

And she just said she'd have him.

Occasionally, when Calhoun had been talking to the Lord about his future wife, he'd asked that God would make her pretty.

He hadn't expected God's plan to include someone so beautiful.

"We have a lot of things to talk about," he finally murmured. Like the ladies weren't standing there staring at them.

He wasn't sure that he could be Mr. Bellamy Levine. He definitely didn't want to be Mr. Bellamy Levine in California. Could he give up everything he had to follow her across the country?

Because she could hardly be Bellamy Levine, movie star, in North Dakota.

And if he was going to give up traveling eight months out of the year in order to be home with his family, he wasn't interested in living with a woman who would have to travel to make movies and be gone just as long.

Her face fell just slightly, but then she lifted her chin. "If God is working it out for us, there really isn't anything to discuss, is there?"

It was a challenge. He wanted to meet it. But there was a part of him that wanted to have everything nailed down, despite the fact that he just talked to his brother, who had confirmed everything that he had been feeling, and now the Piece Makers had admitted that they had been involved as well.

Would God seriously get a whole town involved in finding a mate for him?

Maybe he just didn't like to move so quickly. Or maybe he wasn't used to it. After all, he'd been waiting fifteen years. To make a decision in less than two weeks seemed kind of crazy after waiting so long.

"You're right. If this is God's will, we'll figure something out."

She smiled a little, but her smile seemed sad. He didn't know much about women, but that hadn't been very romantic.

He wasn't really a romantic kind of guy.

Maybe...maybe that was something he needed to change about himself. Or at least something he needed to work on.

After all, if God were giving him someone so caring and beautiful, so very perfect for him and so willing to put herself into what he was doing, whether it was homeschooling three boys or building a cabin or cooking supper, surely the least he could do would be to try to be even a little romantic. He didn't want her to regret being with him.

"Just for the record, before we came to town today, I was really hoping it was God's will. I did ask Him to show me, because... Remember when I told you about getting emotions involved?"

She nodded her head.

"I knew I was at that point. Because... I want to, too."

Her eyes flashed, and her lips tilted up.

"And everything that's happened to me so far today has backed up the idea that finally what I want seems to be what God wants for me too." He grinned. "I always heard that God gives us His best, but I'm not sure I'd ever experienced that until now. If you'll have me?"

His words weren't pretty, and they weren't poetic. Not in any sense of either word, but it made Bellamy smile, and that's the thing that was most important to him.

"If I'll have you? Is that a North Dakota marriage proposal?"

"Maybe." He hadn't been planning on proposing, or maybe he would have done better. "I guess it wasn't a very good one."

"Not to rub it in, but I've had some pretty elaborate marriage proposals. It would almost be true for me to say that I've had marriage proposals that lasted longer than marriages. And I guess, I guess the marriage proposal isn't as important as the character of the man behind it."

"That's one of those lessons you learned?"

She grinned and nodded, remembering their conversation of the previous night.

"Well then, if you've decided you're getting married, maybe you ought to do that before the storm hits," Kathy said, clapping her hands together like it had been settled.

"Maybe the lady wants a nice church wedding," Calhoun said, somehow going from being unsure that this was God's will to kind of liking the idea of getting married this afternoon.

After all, if they were going to be stuck out at the cabin, possibly snowed in, it probably would be better to be married.

And if they were sure that what they were doing was the right thing, he didn't see any point in waiting, even if he did feel like things were going a lot faster than what he expected.

"If we were to get married today, I guess I could say that this was my shortest engagement."

He chuckled. "I'm not sure I appreciate being compared to the last five."

"I'll try to keep that in mind. Although..." She tilted her head. "You come out on top every time."

"I think that's our cue to leave these two alone," Charlene said with authority.

"I need to offer to pay for the damages," Teresa said, her voice not nearly as confident nor loud as everyone else's.

Calhoun figured it probably took a lot for her to have admitted it, since she was typically quiet and sweet.

"We all need to pay for the damages. You are the one who showed us what to cut, but you weren't the only one who caused the problems," Vicki said, stepping closer and putting her arm around Teresa.

"My time is free. If I hadn't already told Rem that, I would do so now. After all, you were doing it for my own good, and..." His eyes went to Bellamy who had stepped closer. He kept himself from moving, even though he wanted to close the distance between them. "I'm pretty happy with the outcome."

"*Now* it's time for us to leave," Charlene said, putting her arm around Teresa and leading her out of the hall. The ladies herded the boys who had all gathered at the end of the hall too, leaving Calhoun and Bellamy alone in the dim, narrow area.

"I hope I'm not pressuring you." Calhoun walked closer and put his hands on her shoulders before sliding them around her back.

She leaned into him easily, wrapping her own arms around him. "And here I was thinking it was the opposite. I don't have to go back to the cabin, although I want to. But I understand it might not be the wisest for us to be stranded together for any length of time."

"Because you can't keep your hands off of me?"

"Maybe." She echoed his earlier answer.

"Can I say the feeling's mutual?"

She tilted her head back and offered him a beautiful smile. "Yes."

That made his smile even lighter, and his chest filled up with all the good things. "You know that unconventional marriage proposal I threw at you just a few minutes ago?"

"Yeah?"

"Did you ever answer it?"

"Yes. I said yes."

They grinned together as his head lowered and she reached up at the same time, and their lips met and he forgot about the ladies and the cabins and the kids and the storm that was coming, and he just thought about how grateful he was that he'd waited, because God had given him more than he ever would have settled for on his own.

Chapter 22

*Stubbornness. I am determined that bad moods and un-
pleasant behavior will not run me off. Oh. Did you mean
something positive? Friendship with each other.
- Mich Arenas from Illinois*

Had she done the right thing?

Bellamy stood beside Cayson's bed, tucking the little boy in and having some major second thoughts.

"Cold feet?" Calhoun's voice in her ear made her hands pause and her eyes blink before she kept going, shrugging her shoulders and shaking her head.

Talk about mixed signals.

"Are you guys our mommy and daddy now?" Cruz asked, his voice sounding a little scared, a lot insecure, and very hesitant.

It cracked Bellamy's heart. Her mom hadn't been a great parent, but at least she'd never wondered who her mom was. Who her parents were. Whether they were coming back.

She answered without looking at Calhoun. "We can be if you want. We're hoping that's what's going to happen. Is that okay with you?"

Cruz nodded, but it was a slow nod, almost as though he really wasn't sure. Maybe he wanted his mom. Of course he probably did.

"You'll always have a place with us. And we'll love you just as much as a mom and dad love their children. But I think there will always be a place in your heart for more than one set of parents, if that's what you get."

"I don't even know who my dad is." Calvin's voice came out softly from his side of the room.

"Me," Calhoun said easily.

Bellamy looked at him, and his face was calm, confident.

She knew, biologically speaking, he actually wasn't, but Calhoun took the boys because he knew what it was like to be abandoned by his mother. And she loved that he was using his past experience in hardship to understand the boys needed someone who wanted, truly wanted, them.

Calhoun had a few more words of reassurance for the boys, and when they fell silent, he assured them that he would talk about it whenever and wherever they wanted to.

He didn't mention that he hadn't heard from Maci since the guardianship hearing, though he'd told Bellamy that earlier that day, and the thought made her bite her lip. It had been a little over a week, but still. That seemed like a long time for a mom to just walk away from her three children and not even care about contacting them or anyone, even to see if they were okay.

They both left the room shortly afterward, with Bellamy walking over to the couch, standing in front of the window, seeing that the snow had started. Little flakes drifting down. They'd get heavier by morning.

"Always thought it was pretty when it snowed. Just something about seeing the random yet choreographed movements of the snowflakes falling down. It's just mesmerizing. Soothing."

She agreed. Just watching the snow, loving the way they swirled but always went down, made her feel a little more settled.

Still, she might have just made a huge mistake.

"I hoped I wasn't pushing you today."

"You weren't." She spoke quickly. Because he hadn't tried to talk her into anything; they'd come to the decision themselves. And then it had just worked out that the pastor was available, and the courthouse had been open, and there was no waiting period in North Dakota. So it worked out.

"Then am I just imagining that you seem to regret it?"

She sighed, deeply, a sigh that came the whole way from her toes and seemed to fill the room. "I guess I hadn't considered how it was going to look to everyone. Here I am again, making a rash decision. Marriage number six. I didn't even have you sign a prenup! My lawyer is going to tell me I'm the stupidest person in the world. My agent will roll her eyes. And...if my assistant were here..." She looked over at Calhoun. "She'd be flirting with you right now probably. Or pushing to handle everything so she could impress you with her newfound industry."

"She'd be wasting her time."

Calhoun hadn't moved. He didn't need to. She could have twenty assistants, and Calhoun would never flirt back. He wouldn't allow himself to be impressed by a fake show of competence. She also knew, beyond the shadow of a doubt, that he would never act like her assistant was more important than she was. Or give her assistant more time and attention.

That was always how it started. Her husband started laughing at her assistant's jokes. Getting excited when her assistant was coming. Sending emails and texts to her assistant.

"I know," she finally said. She couldn't imagine Calhoun having a flirty conversation on social media with her assistant. On Bellamy's own social media page. That's what Houston had done. He'd spent more time interacting with Wanda on Bellamy's social media page than he'd spent interacting with Bellamy anywhere.

Talk about a big red flag.

She sighed again. Calhoun wasn't like that. Calhoun wasn't the kind of person who needed to have a million people groveling at his feet in order for him to feel validated. In fact, he didn't seem to need anyone, but he wanted her.

He'd waited for her.

Years.

She sighed. "You know, I was dreading seeing Houston out with Wanda. I want to hate them both. Just because of the pain they caused me."

"That's natural."

"But it's not right."

"Of course not. Still, you're human."

"But, I've been thinking about how all the things that happened to me led me here. To you."

"God loves me." His smile said that he considered himself a very blessed man.

She returned his smile, but her thoughts were still serious. "I feel like there are lessons in all of that too – lessons in how to handle pain, how to love hard people, how to forgive – I'm still working on that one – that maybe social media is a dumb place to be, anyway, and definitely not a good place for real relationships."

"Can't disagree. It's too easy to hide the bad and only show the good. Even the bad that someone might show is framed in a certain way, deliberately."

"Yeah. It feels real, but that's just an illusion. It's all designed to keep people engaged and make money for the platform you're on."

He nodded, but didn't say much. He'd never been on social media and that seemed like a smart decision. Not that cheating and flirting and pain couldn't happen in real life. But she'd learned things.

And who was she kidding? It was her sixth marriage, and she wasn't even sure they'd made the right decision.

"I'm so sorry. You deserve so much better than me. I don't know why I even agreed to this today."

"That's the problem? You think I deserve better?" He sounded like he couldn't believe it.

"Yeah."

"You're thinking about your exes? Cheaters? Whether or not this would last?"

"All that, I guess." Crazy how he could read her mind. "But that doesn't worry me. Not when I look at you. It's true that there are people in the world like that. It's true that I somehow managed to pick more than my share of them. But you're different. You're not someone who gets excited about the latest new thing. You're not going to look at my assistant and think you need to treat her better than you treat me. You're never going to leave me."

She grinned sadly and looked back out at the falling snow. "I know it's cliché to say it's not you, it's me, but it's true. People are going to flip when they find out I got married again for the sixth time. No prenup. I barely know you. And yet... Just another rash decision."

"I thought you said you thought this was what God wanted."

"I do," she said, adamantly, because she believed it.

"Then it's not a rash decision. It's just you doing what God wants, in God's timing. Even if that timing isn't what the rest of the world thinks it should be. You know God can work fast as well as slow."

"You're right." She'd forgotten all that. "I'm sorry. I guess... I guess I just don't trust myself."

"It's just moment by moment. If the idea of days or weeks or months or years is too hard, just be determined in the next second to do the right thing. Pretty soon, those seconds add up. They become decades, and you've done the right thing for decades. We're young, we can see five decades together, even more. And every second is a choice to build on the last, until you have those five decades. That's what I'm looking for. Two rocking chairs, two old hands twined together, two toothless smiles, two sets of ears that don't hear anything anymore, eyes that can barely see, but hearts that still love. Not the lustful, passionate attraction kind of love, but the self-sacrificial, the putting you ahead of me, the thinking about you, and knowing you better than I know myself, and wanting to do everything I can to make you smile, keep you secure, protect you, and live my life in a way that honors you and glorifies God kind of love. That's how I will love you."

"You should have written your vows. That was beautiful."

"The vows I spoke today are good enough. I promised to love you. To cherish you. To stay no matter how hard things get. All things I plan on doing anyway, although I didn't really like the whole death parting us thing, but I guess it happens."

"What about my career? That might part us?"

It was his turn to sigh, and he, without touching her, turned and stood shoulder to shoulder with her looking out the window. "I guess if you don't want to stay in North Dakota, I'll go where you go."

"Really? You'll...rent a house while I'm on set?"

"Wherever you are is where I want to be."

"What about the kids?"

"I guess I'll be a stay-at-home dad." He looked over at her and grinned a little.

"What if I want something else?"

"Then we'll do what we can do to make it happen."

"What about you?"

"I guess the kind of love I was talking about earlier isn't contingent on what you do. That's the kind of love I want to have for you. Regardless of what you do for me. Because it's not really love if I'm only giving it to you when you do what I want. Or when you reciprocate my kindness or whatever. Or when you initiate it." He grunted. "I'm a pretty shallow person if my quote unquote love is contingent on how you act toward me."

"The kind of love that you were talking about sounded beautiful and like something I would like to do, but... I don't know if I'm mature enough, unselfish enough, to love someone like that."

"No one said you had to."

"I want to."

"Then it's a second-by-second decision."

She liked the idea of only having to do something for a second. Of building the seconds on top of each other. Just one second after another doing the right thing. Making the right decision, and then making herself follow through. For just one second.

"Are you okay if I want to quit acting?"

She turned toward him, and he froze, then slowly faced her.

"Is that what you want?"

She shrugged, but she already knew in her heart it really was. "It's funny, you go to the city because that's where all the opportunities are supposed to be. But I came here, because somehow, deep down, I knew, and I think everyone else does too, that the things that are really important in life aren't found in the city. They're found somewhere where things are slower, where people care, where life isn't about status and prestige, but it's about others."

She gave him an apologetic look. "I guess it took me coming out here, and maybe even Calvin, Cruz, and Cayson, in order for me to see that I was never going to find what I wanted as long as I kept thinking and living for myself."

"Good way to put it." He smiled slowly, took a step closer. His hand came out and threaded into her hair. "You don't need to live for yourself if I'm doing it for you."

That made her smile. "And I suppose if you're living for me, someone needs to live for you."

"Only if you want to."

Funny how someone giving everything to her made her want to return the gesture. Work more, harder, make it a competition to be better.

He stepped closer to her, his other hand moving to rest on her waist, but his smile was a little ironic. "We can talk like that all we want to, but the fact of the matter is there's always going to be hard times. I might be able to guarantee you that the hard times aren't going to be because I'm flirting with your assistant or looking at her and thinking she's amazing, complimenting her on social media in front of the world, and it won't be because I'm cheating on you behind your back, but there will be hard times. It's just a matter of responding to those hard times with character and making the decisions that you know are best for your spouse and that glorify the Lord."

His hand tightened just a little around her waist, and then he said, "I'm not always going to make the right decision." He looked into her eyes. Serious, but also apologetic. "But I want to, I'm going to try to. And I think that's all anyone can ask. To just keep doing better every day."

She nodded, understanding. "So much of what I've done with my life has been about what people think of me. What they think of my performance. What they think about me on social media or in interviews or in my private life. Six marriages. People are going to think I've lost it. And I know I need to stop thinking about what other people are thinking about and focus on the people around me. Because what they think—what *you* think—is far more important."

His smile cut across his face, and he nodded. "That's exactly right. We get so focused, even when we're not famous, on what the rest of the world thinks, the rest of the town. When you live in a small town, you forget that doesn't really matter. It's far more important to be concerned with what your spouse thinks, what your children see at home when no one else is watching."

"Do you think if we have these basics down, we have a chance?"

"I think we have more than a chance. I think we're gonna do it."

She loved him knowing exactly what she was saying. That she'd been talking about if their marriage had a chance.

"You were talking about love earlier, about how it wasn't really all of those lustful feelings, but it was what you do. I agree with that, but I wanted you to know I have the feelings too." She paused, taking a breath because she was scared but also knew what she needed to say. "I love you."

His smile widened, if that were possible. "You beat me to it."

She grinned back at him.

"I love you too. The feelings kind and the serious kind."

She slipped her hand around his neck and tugged, figuring a declaration like that needed to be punctuated with a kiss. Maybe it would lead to more, maybe it wouldn't, but they had the rest of their lives to figure that out.

Chapter 23

Three weeks later, Calhoun was putting the finishing touches on one of the smaller cabins when his phone rang.

He straightened up from the trim work he was doing, looking out the window at his wife and their three boys playing in the snow that still lingered from the storm they had had the night after Bellamy and he got married.

He smiled at the thought. Of Bellamy. Not necessarily of the snow, although he loved that too.

Later this afternoon, he was going to knock off work early and put Christmas decorations up together with the boys. He couldn't believe he'd gone from planning on spending the holidays alone to having a family that put Christmas decorations up together.

Funny how life could turn so swiftly. Often, the fastest turns seemed like the bad turns, but even the boys being dropped in his lap had ended up being one of the very best things that ever happened to him.

Although Bellamy and he might still be together even without the boys, it just felt right to think it was because of them.

Even if there was lingering doubt and unsettled feelings about what would happen when Maci came back.

If she came back.

He looked down before he swiped his phone on. The caller ID read North Dakota State Police.

A premonition gurgled in his stomach, and suddenly his fingers were shaking as he held the phone to his ear.

"Hello?"

"May I speak to Calhoun Powers, please."

"Speaking."

"You have guardianship of three boys with the last name of Stallingston?"

"Yes, sir."

"The mother was killed in a motorcycle accident in Florida last week. We wouldn't have known about the boys, but when we informed the mother, Ms. Stallingston's mother, who was the next of kin, she mentioned you and that you had guardianship." The cop's detached, businesslike voice cracked a bit when he said, "She only mentioned them and you because she wanted us to know she didn't want them."

Wow. A mother and a grandmother who didn't want them. It made Calhoun angry all over again.

"FCS has been doing some digging, and they've been in touch with the court and judge who granted your guardianship. She spoke highly of you but said she wasn't sure what the relationship was between you and the boys. I'm not asking about that, I'm letting you know that your guardianship stands, and if you are expecting Maci to come back, she's not going to. Anything else you have to take up with North Dakota Child Services."

Calhoun stood, quiet, the phone pressed to his ear.

Maci. Gone. Wow.

He didn't really have any feelings toward her, good or bad, except she was the mother of his boys, and she'd been alive and well mere weeks ago.

Now she was gone.

Maybe it made him think of the brevity of life and how things change, just as he'd been thinking. Except...death was so final.

"Was there a man with her?" he finally asked. He didn't figure the boyfriend who had been with her the day she dropped the boys off was the father of any of them, but he had no way of knowing.

"He is deceased as well." The cop's voice was quieter, almost as though he wasn't sure whether that was information he was supposed to disclose or not, but Calhoun was grateful he had. He had no idea what the next steps were, but he'd definitely try to figure out how to get custody of the boys.

In the meantime, he was going to have to figure out how to tell them that their mother had passed and wasn't ever coming home.

The idea was slightly easier since none of them had cried for her since Cayson had the first couple of nights.

The last week or two, none of them had even asked about her, while Calvin, in a private moment, had confided to Bellamy that he didn't want his real mom to come back, because he liked his life here with them.

Regardless, it was a new wrinkle and one Calhoun hadn't really wanted to deal with, although he supposed there was potential for his life to get easier because of it.

"Mr. Powers?"

"Yeah. I'm still here. Sorry. Thanks for calling."

"You're welcome. Normally we pay a visit, but you're pretty far out."

"I understand. Thanks for your time."

The call ended, and Calhoun ran the possibilities over in his head. He wasn't happy about Maci's death. Far from it. But maybe it wasn't as devastating as what could have been. Of course it wasn't.

He marveled again at the way the Lord worked sometimes. Moving the children from Maci's care to his, prompting him to ask for guardianship, having Judge Baylor grant the hearing and the guardianship in the same day. All that served to make today a little easier.

He probably should have asked what they were doing with the body. The boys might want to visit their mother's grave at some point.

Maybe his lawyer could find out. He'd have to talk to his lawyer, but first, he needed to talk to Bellamy, and then they'd need to figure out when they were telling the boys.

He supposed there was no rush. They could have Christmas first.

Regardless, this was one of those things that happened in life that a person just had to face, get through. Choose the best option, and do the best they could, caring more for the people around them than they did for themselves.

Calhoun picked up the last piece of trim and his air gun. He'd tell Bellamy tonight, and they'd make a decision together about what to do about the boys.

Maci's death weighed heavily on his heart, but he smiled anyway. Just because the thought of Bellamy beside him made everything easier. Just like a marriage was supposed to be. Two people walking through life together.

All those years of waiting made being together so much sweeter.

Epilogue

"**I** think we've taken enough time to celebrate our success with Calhoun and Bellamy. It's time to get serious about getting the rest of the single folks in this town married." Charlene didn't look up from the pieces of fabric she was laying out on the table. Four members of the Piece Makers were in the basement of the church in Sweet Water, and, while the quilt they were working on was important, she felt it was even more so to give some nudges in the romance department.

After all, they didn't want their little town to die out.

"That was a pretty big success. Give us time to enjoy the afterglow." Teresa had been especially relieved when their matchmaking had worked. She'd also paid Remington Martinez for all the damages they'd inflicted as soon as Calhoun and Bellamy had said "I do."

"Who's next?" Kathy asked, always up for a matchmaking challenge.

"Gladys Lafrak is turning twenty-five in a few months. She needs to be married to fulfil the stipulations of her inheritance, and her parents are insisting she choose a certain type of man."

Charlene usually appreciated it when parents wanted to be involved in the choosing of their children's mates. Wisdom gained with age could only benefit the younger generations – if they were willing to listen.

"Rich boys. Probably from the east." Vicki didn't have to think about that for long.

"Or California." Teresa snorted. She had no use for any state west of the Rockies.

"Right. And we've known for years that Gladys and Silas are perfect for each other." Charlene's hands kept arranging the blocks of fabric. She wanted to be sure the colors of the quilt were going to look the way she wanted them to before she started sewing. "But Silas doesn't seem to notice her and she only wants to be friends."

"They drag race together at night," Teresa said casually.

"What?" Charlene asked, surprised. How had this been happening and she'd not heard about it?

"The windows in her fancy car are tinted, but they do it out by my son's farm and I happened to be watching my grandchildren the night she got a flat. He got out of the passenger seat and helped her fix it."

"No. Way." Kathy sounded shocked. "Maybe they won't need us."

"They didn't touch each other. They weren't acting like they were a couple or anything."

"I've never seen them together in town," Charlene said thoughtfully. Everyone knew they were friends – good friends, even though they were total opposites – but no one expected them to be anything more. Not just because Gladys's family was rich, and Silas was just a mechanic in his dad's garage, but also because everyone knew Gladys's mother expected her daughter to marry someone who knew which fork to use at a black-tie event and she acted like Silas didn't know he had a thumb.

"It shouldn't be hard. Just a matter of getting them to see each other as romantic interests rather than friends. And maybe figuring out how to get Gladys's mother to...I don't know. See Silas's worth?"

"That's probably not going to happen." Charlene tapped her chin, studying the pattern she'd laid out on the table. "But getting Silas and Gladys to notice each other might be easier if they're already racing together." She hadn't expected that and it was those little God-gifts that made her think she was on the right track. After all, she'd had one of those when Bellamy and Calhoun had been going to stay out at Rem's all by themselves over the holidays. How could she pass up the opportunities that were set in front of her?

"I heard Bellamy is expecting." Vicki's statement broke through the silence that had descended in the basement.

"I hope it's a girl," Teresa said. "Those boys need a sister to give them a little calming influence."

"More likely with three older brothers, a girl is likely to grow up to be a terror."

"Not with Calhoun as her dad. He's a great father. You can see it when he's with his family. He loves and adores them. All of them." Vicki sighed, and Charlene had to agree. It was beautiful to see Calhoun with his family. She could watch them all day.

"It's like I said. We can't rest on our laurels. We need to get moving on the rest of these single folks in town. We'll work on Silas next, just because of Gladys's time constraints."

"That's a good idea. If Gladys ends up married to some rich Easterner –"

"Or a suave Californian."

"Or a Californian," Teresa agreed. "She'll end up leaving Sweet Water."

"She'll end up divorced, too." Vicki said with absolute confidence.

"I agree." Charlene moved two pieces of fabric from one side to the other, arranging them so they fit together. The colors were perfect. "I have an idea for them, but we're going to need some help."

"Help?"

"Yeah. Although the drag racing will make it easier, we're still going to need to do a little manipulating."

"I don't want to destroy any more plumbing or electrical work. That made me feel terrible." Teresa shuddered.

"No property destruction. Just some good, old-fashioned kissing." Charlene looked around at the ladies and grinned. All of them had perked up at the "k" word, as she'd known they would. She refrained from rubbing her hands together. This was going to be fun.

Enjoy this preview of *Cowboy Finding Love,* just for you!

Cowboy Finding Love

Chapter 1

*Communication, understanding, picking your battles, and
never going to bed angry.
- Sharon Marks from the United States*

"It's the Porsche again."

Gladys LeFrak wiggled her fingers—once—at the white handkerchief that weaved out of the cracked driver's side window of the bright red car, waving her own handkerchief from the equally tiny crack in her equally darkly tinted window.

She had no idea if the other driver was even a man or woman.

"They hug the yellow line," Silas Powers reminded her from his position in the passenger seat in a deep, rumbling voice.

His tone always calmed her. Or maybe it was just his personality. Calm. Not "cool."

He didn't strut around, and he was more quiet than any man she knew, but there was just something about him that grounded her.

She'd attempted to race one night without him. Something she would never do again.

"Got it," she said as she pulled her Lexus around beside the Porsche, which was slowly inching forward.

The two-lane North Dakota road stretched out, straight and flat, into the dark distance.

No other cars in sight at one o'clock in the morning. All of her neighbors in the sleepy little town of Sweet Water and surrounding area were sound asleep in their beds.

Nice people. Salt-of-the-earth people, but not the kind of people who stayed out past nine o'clock.

For goodness' sake, even the C-Store in Sweet Water closed at nine. Sometimes when there were no customers, it closed earlier.

The car beside her eased forward in the left lane. She eased up beside it in the right. Although being on the left added just a touch of danger, she would have preferred that position. Having the other car right beside her messed with her mind just a little. It was the optical illusion of it being so much closer than it was when she saw it on the passenger side.

"You have more under your hood than they do. You've got this." Silas's voice broke through the silence of her car.

The thumping of the other car's bass vibrated through their vehicle, the only thing disturbing their quietness. She preferred to race in silence.

On the way home, she'd want the windows down, the radio up.

If Silas had a preference, he'd never said.

The other car inched forward, and she gave it a slight lead while not allowing it to get too far ahead.

Silas was right. She'd beaten this Porsche before, but she couldn't come back from too big of a deficit. She needed to have her reflexes honed.

"Maybe they've done something since the last time we raced."

"That was just last Friday. It would have had to have been something quick and easy. Not enough time to give them more than what you've got."

His words, or maybe just his voice, stilled some of the cramping in her chest, although her heart still beat hard.

She loved the adrenaline surge. Lived for it.

And when the other car smashed the pedal to the floor, waiting a heartbeat or two before releasing the break, squealing the tires and laying a long track of rubber, she was ready.

Her own rubber trail was just as long, and she inched ahead of the Porsche before they covered a quarter of a mile.

She had this, as long as no vehicles came from the other direction.

She'd raced the same Porsche at least seven times, and the one time they met a car, the Porsche hadn't swerved or slowed down.

It was the only time it had beaten Gladys, since she hadn't been able to get within three hundred yards of the oncoming car before she pulled up off the gas and let the Porsche fly by. It had pulled into the right lane just in time, and by the time the car in the left lane had passed Gladys, she was down to a respectable eighty miles per hour.

Right now, the speedometer was tacked out at hundred fifty.

She was probably going much closer to two hundred mph.

But her car handled like a dream. No vibration in the steering wheel, and it hugged the road tightly.

"Dog."

Silas's voice cut through the silence a millisecond before she saw the prairie dog on the road.

Her side.

The Porsche never slowed, but immediately Gladys's foot lifted up from the accelerator, so she was probably only going hundred sixty or so when she hit it.

Just a glancing blow, but it was enough to make her lose control.

"You've got this." Silas's voice came out, comforting her and giving her confidence as the car skidded sideways. She steered into the skid before the rear end fishtailed, and she yanked the steering wheel the other way.

This skid wasn't quite as deep, and she might have been able to straighten out as she accelerated out of it, except the back left tire dropped off the pavement and onto the berm. It must have been a soft spot, because it caught the car, causing it to become airborne and flip.

Later, Gladys assumed that part, and Silas agreed. But she couldn't describe what happened next, other than hearing Silas's voice say, "Keep fighting. You've got it."

Otherwise, she couldn't have said what she did or what happened. All she knew was that the next concrete memory was of them sitting in the right-hand lane, facing in the proper direction, stopped. Four wheels down.

"Impressive," Silas's voice came again.

Her hands gripped the steering wheel, and she sat panting.

They could have died and almost did, and he was complimenting her driving. Like they had just taken a turn around the block.

"I think God had a hold of the wheel. I can't take credit for that."

"Normally I might argue with you, but I think you're right," he said, looking over at her.

She turned her head slowly, shaking her head at the grin on his face.

"People would never know to look at us that you're more addicted to danger than I am," she said with affection.

He grinned, lifting one side of his face in that familiar half smile that was his trademark. For her anyway.

Normally he was serious and quiet and let his actions do his talking, but that grin, and his encouragement, had become something she looked forward to.

"Thanks for staying calm. I know I've mentioned this before, but you help me stay grounded and focused."

"Need to have a purpose for sitting over here."

She smiled a little but wasn't sure exactly whether there might be some hidden meaning in those words.

He'd never asked to drive; she'd never offered, either.

He couldn't afford a car like this, not on a mechanic's salary, but he hadn't ever expressed any interest in owning one, not even a statement that could be interpreted that way.

"Now that I've calmed down a little, it makes me mad that Porsche has beaten me twice now. But both times because of external issues."

"I think that makes you a smarter driver. Sometimes, you need to know when to give up so you can walk away alive."

She grunted, nodding a little. Maybe she didn't care whether she walked away alive. She wasn't afraid, although she had been tonight, maybe not afraid exactly just…just overdosing on the adrenaline that a person gets when they know death is staring them in the face.

It wasn't a fear exactly.

"I guess I don't care if I die," she said, peeling her fingers from the steering wheel. It was true. What was there to live for?

She could do anything she wanted to and had. She'd gone to college, gotten her counseling degree. She'd just finished a master's program and had that diploma, too. But she wasn't sure where she wanted to go now.

The opportunities were greater back when she lived in California. She still had an apartment there but had been staying more and more with her parents because...well, she wasn't sure why.

Their dad had moved to North Dakota because of his business with the oil and needing to be on-site, and her mom, well, she hadn't wanted to move but had gone with her father.

Most of the time, Gladys figured her mom had moved because she was afraid if she wasn't around to babysit her dad, he'd leave her for someone younger and better looking.

He probably would, too. Her dad always seemed like a player to her. At least when she got old enough to know what a player was.

So she'd become one, too. It hadn't been satisfying, but it had given her something to do.

When her dad left California, it had been culture shock to land in North Dakota, and she happened to stop at Silas's family's garage to get a flat tire changed, which they hadn't been able to do, but Silas had just been going on his lunch break, and he'd taken it to drive her to Rockerton and pick her up one.

That had been two years ago, and that had been the beginning of their...was it a partnership?

She wasn't sure. But she'd been casually racing at night, just Silas and her, just for fun.

It had slowly grown into what she'd done tonight. Met up with someone, seemingly randomly, but the same spot she always waited at 1 AM on Friday night, and someone was always there.

Still, there wasn't really anything left for her to do or experience, other than marriage, and she wasn't really interested in that.

Except she kind of had to be. If she wanted to inherit her fortune that had been left to her from her grandmother.

If she didn't marry...she wouldn't inherit her fortune.

Gladys snorted.

"You okay?" Silas asked in the silence of the car.

She realized she'd never moved. Just been sitting there thinking.

"What's the point of life?" she asked, turning her head.

Silas's concerned look didn't ease.

He knew a ton about cars and had learned more since their association. After all, he'd told her over and over that his expertise was with diesel repair, which was different than gasoline engines.

Completely different.

But North Dakota was a big state, though sparsely populated, and lots of people did more than one thing, so Silas had learned about gasoline engines.

And he'd built her what she had.

In the process, she had grown to respect him. He had a lot of wisdom, and he was thoughtful and deliberate about what he did. He didn't make rash decisions, but he enjoyed speed just as much as she did, because he was always ready at 12:45 on Friday night when she picked him up at his house.

"Are you looking for a reason to live? Or are you asking what the point of your life is?"

"Aren't they one and the same?" she asked, looking back out the windshield, feeling stupid for having said it. It wasn't like they hadn't talked about deep things before, because they had, but they had never been personal.

She put on a tough persona to the world, and most of the time, she kept that facade for Silas's benefit as well. She didn't want to appear weak in front of him, of all people. Since he was probably the person she respected most in the world.

He'd earned it. Because with Silas, what a person saw was what a person got.

He didn't put on a big show, not like she was used to. Not just with her family, her parents especially, but with her friends as well. They were all busy trying to look sophisticated and cool and fit in with the crowd. Whatever that was, whatever they had to change about their outer shell in order to cover what they really were and be like everyone else.

Silas was what he was, and he seemed to be very content with that.

"I don't think so. A reason to live might be because you don't want to hurt your family by your death. Or you have things you want to accomplish and aren't ready to go until you've done your best with them. The point of your life is the meaning. Why you're here."

"And why is that?" she asked, almost bitterly.

Nothing she did made a difference. She'd never done one thing for her life to have a point. She wasn't supposed to. She was just supposed to look good and be an accessory, and while she certainly could apply for a position to use her degree, all she could see were endless lines of rich people coming to her complaining about problems that didn't really matter while she sat and listened and asked them how they felt about that and listened some more, then gave them advice that they both knew they weren't going to listen to and took their money.

She'd been to enough counseling sessions herself to know how it worked.

She'd had some vague notion of helping people when she'd gone for her degree, but that had evaporated quickly as she'd listened to her professors and fellow students.

It was about the money. It was always about the money.

Pick up your copy of Cowboy Finding Love by Jessie Gussman today!

A Gift from Jessie

View this code through your smart phone camera to be taken to a page where you can download a FREE ebook when you sign up to get updates from Jessie Gussman! Find out why people say, "Jessie's is the only newsletter I open and read" and "You make my day brighter. Love, love, love reading your newsletters. I don't know where you find time to write books. You are so busy living life. A true blessing." and "I know from now on that I can't be drinking my morning coffee while reading your newsletter — I laughed so hard I sprayed it out all over the table!"

Claim your free book from Jessie!